Professor Tuesday's
AWESOME ADVENTURES IN HISTORY

Book One:
Chief Pontiac's War

JEFFERY L. SCHATZER

mitten press

All inquiries should be addressed to:
Mitten Press
An imprint of Ann Arbor Media Group LLC
2500 S. State Street
Ann Arbor, MI 48104

Printed and bound at Edwards Brothers, Inc., Ann Arbor, Michigan.

10   9   8   7   6   5   4   3   2

Library of Congress Cataloging-in-Publication Data

Schatzer, Jeffery L.
  Professor Tuesday's awesome adventures in history. Book 1. Chief Pontiac's war / Jeffery L. Schatzer.
      p. cm.
  Summary: When an eccentric history professor takes the students from Miss Pepper's class back in time to visit Native American peoples of the woodland tribes, he and one of the students get stuck during Chief Pontiac's uprising in 1763, and the rest of the students must try to rescue them.
  ISBN-13: 978-1-58726-551-8 (hardcover : alk. paper)
  ISBN-10: 1-58726-551-6 (hardcover : alk. paper) [1. Time travel—Fiction. 2. Woodland Indians—Fiction. 3. Pontiac's Conspiracy, 1763-1765—Fiction. 4. Pontiac, Ottawa Chief, d.1769—Fiction. 5. Indians of North America—Fiction.]
I. Title. II. Title: Chief Pontiac's war.

  PZ7.S338Pr 2009
  [Fic]—dc22

                                                    2009002425

Contents

Field Trip

Arrowhead School—Today

Field trip—no school today!

Payton, Kelly, and I were jumping around in excitement when our teacher, Miss Pepper, walked into the classroom. Miss Pepper is a great teacher. She is slender and small, not much taller than the biggest students in our class. What she lacks in size, she more than makes up in energy and spice. She is always bouncing around and making class fun.

Miss Pepper has dark hair with flecks of grey. She usually wears bright colors and has big grey glasses. Our teacher loves pepperoni pizza and collects salt and pepper shakers. That's what I got her for Christmas last year.

"Jesse, it's your turn to lead the Pledge of Allegiance," Miss Pepper said. "It's time to go to Mr. Blackhurst's office."

I'm the best Pledge of Allegiance leader of all time. My mom even said so. When we got to the principal's office, Mr. Blackhurst turned on the sound system and tapped the microphone loudly. Next, he told everyone at Arrowhead School that I would be reciting the pledge.

As I stepped up to the microphone, it made a loud squeaky sound. I put my hands over my ears and giggled. Mr. Blackhurst quickly turned some knobs and the squeaky sound went away.

When it was time, I stood straight and put my hand over my heart as I recited the pledge. Afterward, Mr. Blackhurst read the school announcements. Next week, Arrowhead students are going to be selling popcorn for a fund-raiser. We would be given order forms on Friday. The only other announcement was about our field trip. Miss Pepper's whole class would be out of school for the day.

When we returned to the classroom, everyone was talking about the field trip.

Miss Pepper said it was time to go, so we grabbed our jackets and school bags and went outside. The field trip bus was parked in front of the school. It was soon packed with noisy kids. Some were yelling and shouting. Miguel and Owen were playing rock-paper-scissors in the back. Others were listening to music on MP3 players. Some were digging in their backpacks looking for treats.

Two adults took seats in the front. Miss Pepper was the last one to get on the bus. As she dashed across the parking lot and climbed up into the bus, she slipped on a step and fell into the aisle between the seats. We all gasped. She got up quickly and rubbed her knee.

"We're still going on our field trip, aren't we?" I asked.

"Yes, Jesse, we are still going on our field trip," Miss Pepper said. "I just bumped my knee, that's all."

She brushed off her clothes and flipped the hair out of her eyes. Miss Pepper took another step and almost fell over again. When she looked down, Miss Pepper noticed that she had broken a heel off one of her shoes. The missing shoe heel made her walk funny. She stepped up, then down—up, down, up, down. Her awkward walk made us laugh.

After composing herself, our teacher raised two fingers into the air. It was the Arrowhead School sign for quiet. "Please sit up and pay attention," she said. Nearly everyone sat up straight and looked at our teacher. As usual, Robert was in his own world.

"Robert," Miss Pepper said. "ROBERT!"

Tyrell elbowed Robert in the side. Robert looked up and realized that Miss Pepper was talking to him.

"Take the buds out of your ears and put the game away," Miss Pepper said. Once Robert was done, she announced, "The subject of our field trip today is social studies."

"That's lame," Robert said. "Why don't we ever go on sports field trips?"

Miss Pepper ignored Robert's comment. "We will be visiting the university to learn about a very famous Native American war chief ... Chief Pontiac."

"What-ev," Robert said, rolling his eyes.

"Pontiac?" Rachel asked. "Like the car?"

The teacher smiled. "Why yes, cities, streets, places, buildings, cars, and many other things have Native American names."

"I thought so," Rachel said in her usual know-it-all way. "Sometimes my dad goes to the city of Pontiac."

"What did Chief Pontiac do that was so famous?" Madison asked.

"Professor Tuesday will answer all your questions," Miss Pepper replied. "He is one of the most knowledgeable historians in the country and an expert on Chief Pontiac."

"Great," said Robert, as he slumped in his seat, "another bor-r-ring lecture."

Miss Pepper gave Robert a stern look. "Before we leave, I want to remind everyone to be on their best behavior and pay attention at all times." She thought for a moment before continuing, "Professor Tuesday is a very nice person, and he is very smart. However, you must know that he is a bit different."

"What do you mean, different?" Manuel asked.

"Dude," Robert said, "she's trying to say that the professor is weird."

Some of the kids laughed.

Miss Pepper clapped her hands to get everyone's attention. "That's enough of that," she said. "Professor Tuesday is a brilliant man. It's just that he is a bit peculiar. Sometimes people who are very smart may also have unusual ways."

"Like what?" I asked.

"Well, Jesse," Miss Pepper said, "Professor Tuesday doesn't look like most people. He is also very superstitious." The teacher looked around the bus. "When we meet him, we should all be respectful. I don't want any giggling or whispering. Let's keep our mouths closed and our eyes and ears open."

Miss Pepper turned to Louis. "Why don't you introduce your guest?"

Louis stood up in the aisle of the bus and pointed to the older man who was sitting next to him. "Everybody, this is my grandpa. His name is Mr. La Blanc, but I call him Pops." Mr. La Blanc stood up and waved to everyone.

Miss Pepper then introduced a lady we'd never seen before. "And, this is Mrs. Finch. She teaches geography at the high school. I asked her to come with us today to help us understand the geography of Chief Pontiac's time. Both Mr. La Blanc and Mrs. Finch speak French. That may also come in handy."

Miss Pepper sat down in the front by the driver and the bus chugged off. As we bounced in our seats, most of us were confused about what our teacher had said. We understood how a geography teacher might be helpful. But, why would we need people to speak French to learn about a Native American war chief? And, just how weird was this Professor Tuesday?

Robert didn't seem to care. His ear buds were plugged in and he was blasting the bad guys on his game.

The Professor
Today

Before long, the bus pulled up in front of a big stone building. A wide stairway led up to tall wooden doors that had large metal handles. It was kind of spooky looking. As we stepped inside, our shoes made loud clopping sounds on the hard, shiny floors. Miss Pepper led us down the quiet and empty hallway. All the way, she stepped up then down, up then down, walking in the shoes with one broken heel.

"Is this place haunted?" Tamika asked. "I don't like ghosts."

"The only thing around here that's haunted is your head," Robert said.

Owen and Sim laughed until Miss Pepper stopped in the middle of the hallway and turned to face them. She didn't even need to say anything. Miss Pepper gave them "the look."

We came to another set of big wooden doors. The sign above them read "AUDITORIUM." Miss Pepper took hold of the door handle and then gave the Arrowhead School sign for quiet. "Remember," she said, "be respectful and pay attention." Miss Pepper made a zipper sign across her mouth and put her hands behind her ears. "Remember everyone—mouths closed, eyes and ears open."

"Whoa," we whispered as the door opened. The auditorium was like a giant movie theater. Rows and rows of seats went down to a stage at the front. Long black curtains hung from each side of the stage. The walls were covered with maps, some looking very old. A huge white screen hung from the ceiling. In the very middle of the stage, there was a table with a laptop computer. A projector of some sort hummed softly. Wires of all colors and sizes were plugged into the computer. A small globe sat on the very top of the tangle of wires.

Miss Pepper led us down in front to the first few rows by the stage. She put her finger to her lips. "Sh-h-h," she shushed us. "I will go to see if the professor is ready." She crossed the stage and went behind the curtain. When she returned, a broad smile spread across her face.

"Students of Arrowhead School, it is my pleasure to introduce our distinguished presenter today, Professor Hickamore P. Tuesday." Miss Pepper stepped off the stage and started clapping her hands. We joined in the applause.

We clapped and clapped and clapped, but nothing happened. As the applause died down, we started whispering and mumbling. Miss Pepper gave the Arrowhead School sign for quiet again. We sat in silence as minute after minute went by.

We were getting restless when the curtain on the left side of the stage moved ever so slightly. Eyes peered out—then quickly hid behind the curtain. This happened twice. Miss Pepper was right— Professor Tuesday is a curious fellow.

At long last the professor slowly came out from behind the curtain. He looked at us without saying a word. The professor stared at a ladder that was propped up against the side of the stage. Then he slowly lifted his left leg and took one large step forward, then a second—careful not to step underneath the ladder. His lips moved silently with each step. He seemed to be counting—one, two.

"Weird," said Robert a little too loudly.

Professor Tuesday has a bushy beard. His hair is mostly white and wild looking. A wide bald spot crowns the top of his head. Thick glasses hang low on his nose, and his eyes are constantly moving back and forth. Strange-looking clip-on sunglasses hung on his pocket.

His clothes were funny, too. He wore a white overcoat, something like doctors wear. His name was lettered in cursive on one side. The bulging pocket on his coat was jammed full of pens, pointers, and such. Underneath his coat, he wore a white shirt and a very ugly bow tie. Bright red shoes poked out from under the bottoms of his wrinkled pants.

Professor Tuesday was very different, indeed.

The auditorium was dead quiet. We all jumped when the professor spoke his first words.

"How do you do?"

We didn't know how to answer his question.

The Tuesday Teleporter
University Auditorium—Today

"Today," the professor said, "we're going to learn about Chief Pontiac, the Woodland Tribes of the Upper Midwest, and the rebellion that nearly pushed the British out of North America in 1763." The professor adjusted his glasses up and down before he continued. "We will even go back in time to visit them."

"What?" Dakota asked. "How can we visit people who lived a long time ago?"

Professor Tuesday blinked twice and smiled. "I will take you back in history with my invention, the Tuesday Teleporter." The professor picked up the globe for the class to see. "When I input information into my laptop, this globe creates a teleporter that can take us wherever we want to go—any Tuesday in history. And, it can bring us back safely."

"Ya, right," said Robert.

Professor Tuesday paid no attention to Robert's comment. Instead, he spoke to Mrs. Finch, the geography teacher. "Please go to the map of North America and show us the Mississippi River."

The geography teacher held up a pointer and laid it at the middle of North America along the course of the Mississippi River. The big river almost cut the United States in half.

Professor Tuesday lifted one shoulder then the other before beginning. "Native peoples who lived to the east of the Mississippi River, or to the right of Mrs. Finch's pointer, have come to be known as the Woodland Tribes. They got this name because their villages were usually in deep forests of pine, oak, maple, and birch trees."

"My dad says that the native people of North America lived in houses called teepees," Rachel said. "My dad's a doctor. He knows everything."

"While I am sure that your father is very smart, young lady, teepees were built by Plains Indians. These were tribes who lived west of the Mississippi River," the professor said with a slight smile. "The native peoples of the Woodland Tribes usually lived in shelters called wigwams. Some tribes preferred to build longhouses. Those shelters were as long as one hundred fifty feet."

"Bor-r-ring," said Robert.

Miss Pepper gave him an angry look.

The professor didn't seem to hear what Robert said. Instead, Professor Tuesday bent at the waist. His head hovered over the laptop on the table. He reached out a hand and turned on the computer. "Rather than telling you about the Woodland Tribes, let's visit them."

The professor picked up the globe with both hands. "With your teacher's permission, I'd like to take you back to Tuesday, June 9, 1620."

Miss Pepper nodded her head enthusiastically.

"Get ready to visit a tribe of Wyandotte Indians near Sandusky, Ohio, nearly four hundred years ago."

"Sandusky? I've been to that big amusement park there," Robert said. "This I've got to see."

"Do we have to ride on the roller coasters?" Tamika asked. "I'm afraid of roller coasters."

The professor smiled. "Don't worry, Miss, we're going back to a time before there were Europeans in the area. So, there won't be any roller coasters, either."

Professor Tuesday went back to work on his laptop. He mumbled and hummed to himself as he tapped at the keys. When he was done typing, he lifted his glasses slightly and studied the screen before attaching a cable. The cable was then connected to the globe—his Tuesday Teleporter. Before hitting the enter key on his laptop, the professor's eyes grew narrow and his voice took on a serious tone.

"You must all pay close attention to what I say," the professor began. "If you talk or wiggle around, we may be discovered. If you wander off, you could even be captured."

We all shook our heads in agreement. Then the professor told everyone to stand in a line and hold hands. We quickly gathered at the front of the stage and held hands. Sim didn't want to hold Ashley's hand, but Miss Pepper made him do it. Then Miss Pepper took her place at the front of the line.

The professor took his sunglasses from his coat pocket, put them on, and flipped them down. Then he raised two fingers high in the air above his laptop. "Prepare yourselves to travel back in time." Then he came down on the enter key of his laptop with both fingers.

The globe started to rattle and shake as it rose slowly into the air. Squares of blue, red, and white lights started shooting out of it and began circling the room. They formed pieces of light clouds that got larger and larger as they spun faster and faster. A low humming sound grew and grew. A wind came out of nowhere and blew our hair around as the lights tumbled and spun around us.

"I'm going to puke," Payton shouted.

"I don't like this," Tamika said over and over.

"Everyone relax," the professor shouted above the noise. "The teleporter is forming."

Suddenly, we heard a loud "pop." All the wind, lights, and sounds stopped. A green gob that looked like jelly hung in the air next to the professor. The gob was about as big as a bathtub.

"Is that it?" Robert asked.

"Everything in time," said the professor. "Let me check to see if it is safe for us to travel."

Professor Tuesday stuck his head into the gob of green jelly. After a time, he pulled his head out and looked around at us. There wasn't even a speck of jelly on him.

"It's safe, now we can travel back in time."

He took Miss Pepper's hand and we all followed them into the gob of green jelly. That's when the fun ride started.

When we entered the Tuesday Teleporter, we were surrounded by swirling colors as we tumbled through space.

"Now I'm really going to puke," yelled Payton.

"Me too," said Tamika.

I was too amazed to be scared. After a few moments, the whole class was standing in the middle of some high grass. The professor motioned for us to crouch down.

The Wyandotte Tribe

Sandusky, Ohio—
Tuesday, June 9, 1620

The ride through time made us all very dizzy. Kim and Kelly nearly fell over. Manuel stumbled to his knees. Pablo lost his glasses, but he found them in the grass at his feet. The class was standing in tall weeds along a shoreline. The nearby lake was so big we couldn't even see the other side. The forest behind us was thick with trees and brush. A long shelter stood nearby. Smoke rose from the far side of the shelter, and we could smell food cooking. Ahead, we could see the outline of a small village.

"Smells good," Miguel whispered. "I'm hungry."

"Dude, you're always hungry," said Robert.

"Sh-h-h," Natalie said in a quiet voice. "Remember what the professor said. I don't want to be captured."

The village was very quiet. Suddenly we saw some native children chasing each other in and around the shelter. The children wore clothes that looked to be made out of animal hides. They weren't wearing shoes. Their bare feet kicked up dust and dirt as they ran. It looked like they were playing a game. But, I couldn't figure out what kind of game it was. They laughed and shouted as they ran.

When I go to the movies, I always see native people riding horses. So I looked around for horses, but I didn't see any. As the children ran and played, dogs nipped at their heels.

Several women and older children were working in a nearby clearing. Everyone had dark brown skin and black hair. The women had moccasins on their feet and wore dresses made of animal skins. They tended plants and pulled weeds, just like my dad and mom do in our garden at home. The tools they used appeared to be made from stones. Some had crude wooden handles.

As we watched the garden work, we noticed several native men walking toward the village. They looked kind of scary to me, but each man had a cool haircut. Brushy hair stuck up in a narrow strip in the center of their heads with the sides of their heads shaved closely. The men held spears, clubs, and bows and arrows, while a group of older boys walked behind them carrying thin branches loaded with fish.

As the men and boys approached, several women came out from the village to greet them warmly. The women began preparing the fish as the men sat near the shoreline and talked. I could clearly hear them talking, but I couldn't understand a word they said.

Professor Tuesday looked around and waved slightly to get our attention. Then he pointed at a section of beach away from where the men sat. Two men were building a canoe. A frame of branches in the shape of a canoe was upside down. The men were putting a large section of tree bark on the bottom. They had a small fire near the shore. A pot rested on the coals. We watched them work for a long time until something else caught our attention.

A huge black cloud began forming on the horizon over the lake. The men sitting on the beach and the canoe makers stopped what they were doing and watched as the cloud gathered and grew. It stretched from the north to the south and got bigger and bigger and bigger. But, we soon realized it was no cloud—clouds don't make noise.

Tamika and a few others started looking scared. We could hear the sound of bird wings. What we thought was a cloud was actually a flock of birds. Soon it nearly covered the sky. As we watched, we were startled by a different noise.

"A-a-a-CHOO!" Owen sneezed loudly.

The native people looked in our direction. The men whooped, held their weapons high, and ran toward us.

A frightened look crossed the professor's face. He turned to us and shouted, "Everyone hold hands, quickly."

We clutched hands and the professor led us through the green jelly once again. Soon we were gathered up in a whirl of colors and sounds. A few moments later, our entire class was back in the auditorium.

"Whew," said the professor as he wiped his forehead, "that was close."

"Sorry," Owen sniffed. "I've got allergies."

The professor's scared look turned to relief. "That's okay, young man, all that matters is that we got back safely." The professor flipped up his sunglasses, then turned to our teacher. "Miss Pepper, would you please count your students and guests. I just want to make sure that everyone made it back."

Our teacher went to work counting heads. "Everyone made it back safely, Professor."

"That was pretty cool," Tyrell said. "Can we do it again?"

"We'll see," Professor Tuesday replied.

"My mom always says 'we'll see,'" Robert said. "That means 'no.'"

Payton and Kelly looked disappointed. "Can we do it again, Professor ... please?" Kelly whined.

"I believe we can," the professor said. "But, before we travel back in time again, let's talk about what we saw."

Lessons from the Wyandotte
University Auditorium—Today

Professor Tuesday brushed his beard with his fingers as he spoke. "Well, what did you see when we visited the Wyandotte?"

"It was pretty cool," Robert said, "but I didn't see an amusement park."

We all laughed.

Professor Tuesday laughed, too. "That's correct. We visited a site that was very close to where a major amusement park is today."

Rachel raised her hand and spoke without being called on by the professor. "I saw a really, really big teepee." She held her arms wide to emphasize her point.

"What you saw, my dear, was a longhouse," the professor said. "Most Wyandotte Indians lived in longhouses. Remember what I said before? Plains

Indians lived in teepees. Woodland Indians lived in wigwams or longhouses."

"That's right, Rachel," Nathan said. "YOU don't know everything."

"That's enough of that," Miss Pepper scolded. "Now, what else did we see?"

"What were those birds?" Tamika asked. "They scared me—there were so many."

The professor nodded at Tamika. "That's a very good question. The birds you saw were passenger pigeons. They would travel in flocks that were a mile or so wide and up to three hundred miles long."

"No kidding?" Payton asked.

"No kidding," the professor said as he adjusted his glasses. "Some scientists think that there were up to five billion passenger pigeons at one time. Their flocks were so large that they could cover the entire sky for hours, sometimes days.

"Cool," Robert said. "So, how come I've never seen a flock of birds like that before?"

"Passenger pigeons are extinct in our time," Professor Tuesday replied. "The last wild passenger pigeons died over a hundred years ago. It appears as though they could not survive as human populations increased in North America."

We all thought about what the professor said.

"Now, what else did you notice during our trip?"

Sim spoke up suddenly, "The men caught fish. My dad and I go fishing all the time. But we use rods and reels and stuff. I didn't see the men carrying any tackle boxes or fishing stuff."

"Excellent, excellent," the professor said. "Most native tribes fished in rivers and lakes, but they didn't use the same equipment most fishermen use today. They usually used handmade nets, traps, and spears." The professor raised one hand, then the other, before he spoke again. "Now, if you wanted fish for supper tonight but didn't catch any, what would you do?"

"I'd go to a restaurant or buy some fish at the grocery store," Miguel answered.

The professor clapped his hands twice. "Did anyone see a grocery store or a restaurant?"

We all shook our heads "no."

"Native peoples lived off the land," the professor said. "They were in a constant struggle for survival. If they didn't catch fish or game for food, people went hungry. In fact, it wasn't uncommon that entire villages of Native Americans starved to death. So, everyone worked to gather food. Women planted crops and cooked. The men were excellent fishermen. They would also hunt for turkey and deer—sometimes they even hunted for bear."

"I didn't see any guns," Owen said. "How would they kill bear?"

"Most Native Americans didn't have guns in 1620. They would hunt for bears with spears, traps, and bows and arrows. Can you imagine that?"

Tamika wrinkled her nose. "Bears scare me."

"Dude, did they play any sports?" Robert asked.

The professor's eyes brightened at the question. "Why, yes they did. And, what is your name young man?"

Robert looked around before he spoke. Miss Pepper nodded her approval. "My name is Robert."

"Well, Robert, I don't know what those children were playing in the village today. I would guess that they were playing something like tag. But, one of the most popular games native people played was very much like what we know as lacrosse. They used long-handled nets to pass a ball up and down a very long field to score a goal. Native American children even had toys. One popular toy was a doll that was usually made out of corn husks."

"Wow," said Robert sarcastically, "that sounds like fun."

Miss Pepper gave him a cross look and shushed him.

The professor paid no attention. He stroked his white beard, adjusted his glasses, and thought aloud. "Now, where was I?"

"You were telling us that Native American men hunted and fished for food," Ashley said.

"Oh, yes, yes," said the professor. "Everyone had to work. Women and children had many important jobs. In many tribes, women planted gardens, raising vegetables such as squash, pumpkins, and corn—which they called maize."

Sim made a yucky face when the professor mentioned the word *work*. Those around him cupped their hands over their mouths to keep from laughing out loud.

I raised my hand, and the professor called on me. "Professor, how come the men got to catch the fish but the women had to clean and cook them?"

The professor thought a time before he spoke. "Native men and women had different jobs. Their survival depended on lessons and skills that were passed on from generation to generation. Fathers taught sons how to make canoes, clubs, spears, nets, bows and arrows, and such. They showed them how to hunt and fish. Mothers taught their daughters how to care for the village, to cook, and to plant and harvest. Only men could be chief of the tribe—however, women usually chose the person who was to become chief."

"Hey! Hey!" Kelly said excitedly, waving her hand high in the air. "I saw some guys building a canoe or something."

"Yes," the professor said. "The Wyandotte were excellent canoe builders. It was much easier to travel over the water than it was over the land. So, canoe building was an important skill."

"What were they cooking in the fire near the shore?" Pablo asked.

"You are very observant," the professor said. "The canoe builders were probably heating tree sap to use for glue or to seal holes in the bark."

The professor looked around the room. "Now, what else did you see or hear?"

"What language were they talking?" Louis asked. His grandpa smiled at the question.

"Another good question," the professor noted. "Your class is very smart, Miss Pepper. The Wyandotte spoke a language that was much like the Iroquois. Other tribes in the Midwest spoke a language known as Algonquin."

The professor scratched his head. "Did you see anything else?"

"I know! I know!" Natalie said. "The men had really cool haircuts."

"Yes, young lady, they did," answered the professor. "Many believe that they wore it that way so their hair wouldn't get in the way of the bow strings when they shot arrows. Sometimes the men would wear porcupine quills or feathers in their hair."

The professor waited for a few moments before speaking again. "The native people in North America had very hard lives. Tribes would fight each other for food or hunting lands. For centuries very little changed to make the lives of Native

Americans easier or better. However, big changes came when the first Europeans arrived."

Once again, Professor Tuesday turned to his laptop. "Let's take another trip into history," said the professor. "This time we'll go to Wisconsin in 1720 ... a hundred years later than our visit to the Wyandotte in Ohio. We'll see how some of the first Europeans visiting the Upper Midwest changed the lives of the Native Americans they met."

The professor flipped down his sunglasses and chuckled before he pressed enter on his laptop. "This time, let's try not to sneeze."

We lined up once again, and in a matter of moments the lights of the Tuesday Teleporter spun around the room. After the professor stuck his head into the green goo to take a look around, we eagerly followed him through.

The French

Fort La Baye, Wisconsin—
Tuesday, July 2, 1720

Our class arrived in a small clearing in the woods. Just beyond us was a meadow with a river running through it. On the other side of the river was a fort made of logs. I saw one like it at the museum.

"Wow," said Robert softly. "Check out that fort!"

Nearly everyone turned and shushed him.

It was a hot, steamy day in the wilderness. The quiet was powerful. There were no sounds of motors or other city noises. No cars, trains, or airplanes could be heard. The sky was clear and blue. Mosquitoes buzzed in our ears and a bird made a racket over our heads.

Professor Tuesday cautiously looked around. His eyes searched the entire area thoroughly before he turned and whispered a reminder to us. "Watch carefully, but keep quiet and try not to move around."

Owen started making sneeze noises again, but he held his nose with his fingers. The professor smiled at him and mouthed the words *good job*.

Soon a canoe slipped silently down the river. It was being paddled by a Native American man and woman. As it approached the fort, a soldier walked out the gate and waved a greeting. The people paddled the canoe up to the bank near the fort and climbed out. The man and woman carried armloads of furs and hides into the fort. The soldier welcomed them and helped them carry their goods.

"Is that all there is to see?" Dakota whispered.

Professor Tuesday put his fingers to his lips to quiet her.

After a short time, the natives came out of the fort with a different soldier. The native man was carrying a long gun. The woman took a seat on the ground by the gate of the fort while the men walked to the far side of the clearing. The soldier began showing the native man how to load and fire the gun. The man raised the gun to his shoulder. Then his body jerked back and smoke came out of the barrel. A moment later we heard the sound.

"Click, BOOM!" Nearly everyone in the class jumped. Our eyes were frozen wide open as the sound of the gun echoed through the clearing. Birds rose up all around us and cackled as they climbed into the sky. Squirrels chattered loudly, scolding with all their might.

The native man shouted and shrieked with joy while the soldier nodded his approval. They reloaded and shot the gun a few more times before returning to the fort. Both the woman and the man went back inside with the soldier. When the couple came back out, they were carrying the gun, a small wooden barrel, and several bulging cloth bags. Even though it was a hot day, the woman had new blankets draped over her shoulder.

Once the canoe was loaded, the man and woman paddled off up the river. We could hear them saying their good-byes to the soldier, but we were too far away to understand exactly what was being said. It sounded like a different language than the Wyandotte had spoken.

After they left, the soldier went back inside the fort.

"A BUG! A bug is crawling on me!" Tamika cried. She jumped up and down, shaking her hands and trying to brush the bug off.

Miss Pepper went to Tamika quickly to quiet her. Professor Tuesday looked around to make sure no one had heard her cries.

"That was close," the professor whispered. "We were lucky. I don't think anyone heard or saw us. Let's settle down for a while. There's something else I want you to see here. Please, no more noises or movement, it could be dangerous."

We stayed still and quiet behind some low brush in the clearing to make sure we wouldn't be discovered. Nothing happened at the fort for a long time. Then Nathan spotted something.

"Look," Nathan whispered as he pointed to a bend in the river.

I heard it before I saw it. A large canoe was gliding through the water toward the fort. At least ten men were paddling. I was surprised to see that they weren't Native Americans. Some of the men wore brightly colored stocking caps. Others wore rags on their heads. Big bundles wrapped in blankets and animal hides filled their canoe.

They sang in deep, loud voices as they paddled. Nearing the fort, one of the men cupped his hands around his mouth and shouted, "Bonjour le fort!"

Louis's grandpa whispered, "They're speaking French."

The professor nodded and pointed toward the fort. "Keep watching."

Several soldiers came running out of the fort to meet the travelers. They greeted each other warmly. Everyone helped to carry the bundles from the canoe inside the fort.

The professor turned slowly to face us. "It is time to go back now. Let's line up and hold hands."

When we walked through the green jelly portal, Owen lost his shoe and tripped. When he came through the teleporter, he fell face first onto the stage and his shoe was gone.

"Hey," Owen said as he looked up from the floor. "I've got to go back. I lost my shoe."

"Sorry," said Professor Tuesday, "the Tuesday Teleporter cannot go back to the same place twice in one day. I've programmed it that way for safety reasons."

"Ya," said Robert, "some native dude is going to find your shoe and wonder what kind of animal left something that smelled so bad."

Owen blushed as the class laughed.

The French People and the Woodland Tribes

University Auditorium—Today

Professor Tuesday took two giant steps toward the front of the stage. After he flipped up his sunglasses, he put his hands behind his back. "Let's talk about what you just saw."

We all wiggled in our seats and talked about how cool it was to go back in time again. As we chattered, the professor cleaned his glasses on his white coat, first one lens then the other. Then he held up two fingers just as Miss Pepper did.

"Tell me what you saw."

"There was a cool fort, just like in the movies," Natalie said.

"You just visited a French trading outpost called Fort La Baye, in 1720. The very place you were standing is now downtown Green Bay, Wisconsin."

Mrs. Finch went to the map and pointed out the location of Green Bay and Fort La Baye.

"That's where the Green Bay Packers play football," Robert said excitedly. "I love football."

Professor Tuesday chuckled aloud. "Yes, Robert, there is a professional football team in Green Bay, Wisconsin, today. But what you just saw was nearly 300 years in the past. What did you see on our trip back in time just now?"

"The first people I saw were Native Americans arriving at the fort in a canoe," Manuel said.

The professor smiled. "Very good, you saw people who wanted to trade with the French. You see, French missionaries and explorers traveled up the Mississippi River and throughout the Great Lakes region. These explorers included La Salle, Nicolet, Marquette, and Joliet. As the French came to the Upper Midwest, they built several forts like La Baye that were mostly trading posts."

Louis climbed up in his seat. "So that's why they were talking French, like my grandpa said."

"Right you are, young man," the professor replied. "Because of their explorations and trading outposts, the French believed they had claim to the lands of the Woodland Tribes. At the same time, the British believed that they owned the same land."

"Seems to me that the land really belonged to the native people," Louis noted.

"Ah, very good—an excellent observation," said Professor Tuesday.

"It is important to understand that Native American cultures didn't believe that land could be 'owned.'" The professor folded his hands in front of his face before continuing. "However, the French and British both claimed to own the land that was inhabited by these native people. All of these conflicting beliefs eventually led to war."

The professor looked around the auditorium. "So, what was going on back at Fort La Baye?"

"The native dude bought a gun," Robert said.

"Excellent, excellent," said the professor. "Native Americans often traded hides and furs for other goods. That was the purpose of these outposts. Animal skins were very popular back in Europe for hats and clothing. Trading gave the native people new technology ... like guns and tools. This new technology helped them to be more efficient hunters and providers. Unfortunately, this same technology also made them more reliant on the Europeans for tools, guns, gun powder, lead balls, and repairs."

"My dad said that guns are bad," Rachel said.

The professor took off his glasses and rubbed his eyes. "Many people don't like guns, young lady. However, if you have to rely on hunting to survive, guns can be very important tools."

Manuel raised his hand. "The native people carried a small barrel and bags of stuff to their canoe."

"Very good," said Professor Tuesday. "The wooden barrel was probably full of gun powder. The bags could have contained lead balls for the gun, as well as food and other necessary items."

"So, it was good that the Native Americans could trade for stuff," Nathan said.

"Well, yes and no," said Professor Tuesday. "Trading helped both the French and the native people."

The professor thought for a moment before continuing. "At this point, it is important for all of us to understand that the native people in North America had their own traditions and beliefs that weren't always understood by the Europeans. For example, they had a long tradition of gift giving. A chief's power was known by his generosity. The French understood this custom and often gave generous gifts to visiting chiefs. As time went by, most Native Americans developed a strong relationship with the French. In fact," the professor added, "many came to refer to the king of France as their 'father.' There was more than one bad side to this relationship, however."

"What do you mean 'bad side'?" asked Kelly.

"Well," said Professor Tuesday. "If trading and gift giving were to be suddenly taken away, the native people would suffer greatly. They may not be able to get powder and ammunition for their guns and other supplies they needed. Native people had come to rely on trade for their survival. So, their relationship with the Europeans was risky."

The professor took two steps to the side. "In addition, Europeans had many diseases and illnesses that were unknown to the Native Americans. Sicknesses that were common to foreigners were devastating to the native people. For example, many native people died from smallpox, a disease that was carried to North America by the Europeans."

"Who were those guys in the big canoe?" Owen asked.

Professor Tuesday pointed to Louis's grandpa. "I would be willing to guess that Mr. La Blanc can tell us who those men were."

Louis smiled broadly as his grandpa rose and spoke. "They were French-Canadian voyageurs," Mr. La Blanc said. "Louis and I are both descendents of brave men like them."

"Tell the class what the voyageurs did," the professor said.

Mr. La Blanc cleared his throat before speaking. "*Voyageur* is a French word that means 'traveler.' These men would travel, often by canoe, to trading outposts. They would trade food and supplies for furs and hides. The work of the voyageurs was dangerous and difficult. They paddled their canoes for as much as fourteen hours a day and at a strong pace over treacherous waters. Voyageurs also carried heavy loads of supplies and furs over land." Mr. La Blanc smiled as he continued. "From time to time, they were even ordered to carry ladies and gentlemen over land so their feet and clothing wouldn't get muddy."

"No way," Robert laughed.

"It's true," Mr. La Blanc replied.

The professor took two giant steps back to his laptop. "You have learned a great deal already," he said. "Are you ready to learn more?"

"Y-E-E-E-S!" we all shouted together. The whole class was having fun with history.

Conflict
University Auditorium—Today

"I need to explain a few things before we travel back in time again," Professor Tuesday said as he entered data into his laptop. "As the French built more and more trading posts throughout the Midwest, the British grew angry." The professor raised his eyebrows twice before continuing. "Remember what I said before? The British believed that they owned the land in North America. In 1754, war broke out between the two countries."

"Was that the French and Indian War?" asked Miss Pepper.

"Why yes, Miss Pepper," the professor said with a big smile. "It was the French and Indian War, indeed."

The professor sat on the edge of the table on the stage. "Most Native American tribes in the Midwest took up sides with their friends the French. As I said before, many natives called the French king their 'father.' And they were very, very loyal to him. A few tribes, like the Mohawk, sided with the British. As in all wars, many lives were lost on both sides. The war ended with the Treaty of Paris, signed in 1763. The French surrendered to the British and gave up their claims to what was called 'New France.' That included all land in the United States east of the Mississippi, outside New Orleans."

Mrs. Finch pointed out the area on the big map.

"Oh, Professor," said Miss Pepper, "can we go to Paris to see the treaty signed? I've always wanted to visit Paris."

The professor shrugged his shoulders twice and chuckled. "I'm sorry, but I think the treaty was signed on a Saturday. The Tuesday Teleporter only works on Tuesdays and only goes back to Tuesdays in history."

"Oh," the teacher said. She looked disappointed. "I suppose that's true."

"Now, where was I?" the professor asked himself. "Yes, yes, the Treaty of Paris—the peace treaty that ended the French and Indian War. Under the terms of the agreement, nearly all the land that had been claimed by the French was turned over to England. British troops quickly took over the forts and trading posts that had been occupied by the French."

Professor Tuesday thought for a moment or two before continuing. "Even though the British won the war, most native people stayed loyal to the French. Many thought their French 'father' was just sleeping and would awaken to save them. However, the British had other ideas. And, they treated the native people differently than the French had. Problems started right after the war was over.

"What do you mean?" Madison asked.

"He means the British were nasty and the Native Americans weren't happy about it," said Robert.

"Well," said the professor with a chuckle, "I don't think that *nasty* is the word. For one thing, the British didn't believe in giving gifts like the French did. This was no small matter. The native people had come to rely on gifts of food, guns and ammunition, blankets, and so on for their survival. As more and more people moved onto native hunting lands, game became scarce. The British refusal to give gifts caused many of the tribes to nearly starve.

"That's terrible," Sim said.

The professor stroked his long beard as he thought. "Many British leaders considered the Native Americans to be savages rather than people who should be respected and treated with dignity."

"That's bogus," said Robert. "It was their land to begin with, wasn't it?"

"True, true," said Professor Tuesday. "But remember, the British suffered many losses to the native people during the French and Indian War. They believed that the Native Americans could and should take care of themselves without reliance on gifts. Still, some of their attitudes were just plain wrong."

"Can you give us an example, Professor?" Miss Pepper asked.

Professor Tuesday thought for a moment. "Major Henry Gladwin was the British commander of Fort Detroit. Gladwin did not approve of giving gifts. Native people talked to him about their need for gifts of food and other supplies. But, Gladwin felt that the Native Americans were begging, and he refused to help them."

The professor rolled his eyes before continuing. "Many Native Americans were upset by this treatment. Anger boiled over in one particular Native American chief, the war chief widely known as Pontiac."

"Can we meet Chief Pontiac?" Kim asked.

"We'll see," said the professor.

"Did Chief Pontiac live in Pontiac, Michigan?" Miguel asked.

"He spent a great deal of time in the general area," the professor replied. "Pontiac's father came from an Ottawa tribe that was located near what is Detroit today. His mother was from an Ojibwa tribe from the area of Saginaw Bay."

Mrs. Finch pointed out the areas of Michigan as the professor mentioned them.

"Chief Pontiac was one of the most famous Native American leaders to lead a battle against the British."

"What made him so famous?" Payton asked.

The professor clapped his hand twice and took two long steps toward the table on the stage. "Many Native American tribes were angry with the British. As Chief Pontiac expressed his anger against British treatment of his people, his influence spread throughout the Upper Midwest, including Illinois, Indiana, Ohio, Pennsylvania, Wisconsin, and Michigan. There were many, many tribes living in this region, such as the Potawatomi, Ojibwa, Wyandotte, Miami, Illinois, Delaware, Kickapoo, Winnebago, Sauk, Fox, Seneca, Shawnee, Tuscarawas, among others."

"I didn't know there were that many different tribes," Sim said.

"Those are just some of the major tribes in the Upper Midwest, young man," the professor noted before continuing. "Chief Pontiac hated the way his people were being treated. Years before, the British promised not to settle on native lands that were west of the Allegheny Mountains. But, the European peoples seemed to ignore their promises. As the British troops took over the French trading posts, they built many settlements. For these and other reasons, Pontiac called the British liars."

"They were liars, weren't they?" Louis asked.

"That is up to you to decide," the professor replied. "European cultures and Native American cultures were very different from each other. So, there was a lot of misunderstanding on both sides. Still, the British continued to move and settle in what was known as the frontier—even though they had promised not to.

The professor got up from the table and went back to his laptop. "Pontiac was also greatly influenced by a Delaware Indian, a Native American holy man named Neolin. In 1761, Neolin had a vision."

"A what?" Robert asked.

"A vision," the professor answered. "We don't know if his vision was a dream or just a strong idea. Anyway, in his vision he saw evil being brought to the native peoples by the white Europeans. Pontiac believed the vision meant that it was his job to drive out the whites by making war on them."

Professor Tuesday went behind the curtain and pulled out a small camouflaged shelter. Then he placed a webcam and a microphone headset on his bald head. "The next trip is going to be too dangerous to take you along. Mr. La Blanc has agreed to help me. I won't be able to hear anyone except for Mr. La Blanc. However, you'll be able to hear and watch everything on the screen here in the auditorium. I've set the timer on my teleporter to automatically shut down in an hour. I should be back well before then."

I turned to see Mr. La Blanc. He was wearing the same kind of microphone headset as Professor Tuesday.

The professor adjusted his instruments and fiddled with his laptop. Then he flipped down his sunglasses once again. "I will be going back to 1763 and visiting what is now Detroit, Michigan. Chief Pontiac is preparing to hold a meeting with other war chiefs from the region. He wants these chiefs to join him in war against the British."

The professor raised two fingers high into the air over his laptop. "Now stay in your seats, please."

"I don't like the bright lights," said Tamika.

"Then close your eyes," the professor replied.

Even through our closed eyes, we could see the movement of light and hear the low hum as it grew louder and louder.

With all the lights and commotion, no one heard Robert say, "Wait, I'm going, too."

When we opened up our eyes, he had already jumped through the Tuesday Teleporter.

The Ecorse Council

Detroit, Michigan—
Tuesday, April 26, 1763

An image slowly appeared on the screen in the auditorium.

Native men were building a shelter in a small clearing next to a river. Strong branches held the animal-hide roof in place. The shelter had no sides. A fire crackled and blazed. Thin wisps of smoke drifted on the still air. Three men were talking while others worked on the shelter.

"The professor and his equipment are hidden in the woods nearby," Mr. La Blanc spoke up. "The Native Americans are speaking French. I will translate for you."

The sound of Professor Tuesday's whispered voice came over the speakers in the auditorium. "Chief Pontiac came from this very area. No one knows exactly when he was born, but he's about forty-five years old at this time."

The three native men near the shelter were talking loudly. The professor continued in a whisper, "The man facing us is Pontiac. He called all the war chiefs from nearby tribes to a council meeting that will be held tomorrow on this very spot.

Mr. La Blanc listened carefully to the conversation. "Pontiac is calling for war against the British. He is using his anger and the words of Neolin to convince the other chiefs to join him in battle."

The professor added, "The other men with Pontiac are Chief Ninivois of the Ottawa and Chief Takay of the Wyandotte."

Pontiac held up what looked to be a long tobacco pipe. "Look," said Mr. La Blanc. "Chief Pontiac is explaining how he plans to visit Fort Detroit to do what is called a 'peace pipe' dance. The dance will be a trick. Pontiac and his warriors plan to enter the fort to see how it is defended, so they can attack it at a later date."

The professor moved the webcam for a better view of the three chiefs.

Mr. La Blanc listened carefully to the conversation before translating. "Pontiac is telling Ninivois and Takay that he will be sending messengers with war belts to other woodland tribes."

Professor Tuesday's voice squeaked with excitement. "This is very, very interesting. War belts are usually made of red cloth or beads. These belts are used to invite tribes to join in battle. If a chief accepts a war belt, the tribe will go to war."

What happened next made everyone in the auditorium gasp. The native workers noticed something and took off on a run toward the professor's shelter, whooping and shouting. Professor Tuesday, shaking in fear, tried to follow the action with his camera. Everything was happening too fast. Before long, their actions became clear. The warriors returned to the shelter holding something. No, they were holding someone.

They had Robert.

"Oh, no! Oh, no, no!" whispered the professor.

Robert kicked and screamed, trying to get away. The warriors held him tightly. "Help, Professor," Robert cried out. "They got me."

Miss Pepper ran to the stage—up, down, up, down. She pointed her finger at the screen and shouted, "Robert, you get back here this very minute." Slowly she turned and faced the class, her hand over her mouth. Her eyes were wide with fear. Everyone sank into their seats, even Mrs. Finch.

Miss Pepper straightened herself. "Class, we must remain calm. I am sure that Professor Tuesday will do something." We couldn't see that she was crossing her fingers behind her back.

The professor turned the webcam around so that it showed his worried face. "This is not good."

Professor Tuesday tapped the side of his head with two fingers as he thought. "I'll try talking to Chief Pontiac. Maybe, just maybe, he will let Robert go."

The professor swallowed hard. "The teleporter will shut down in a few minutes. If I'm not back with Robert, you will have to find us somewhere in history. Do you understand?"

Miss Pepper nodded her head "yes" even though Professor Tuesday couldn't see her. Mr. La Blanc spoke to Professor Tuesday through the microphone. "We understand. Good luck."

"When you turn my laptop on, all you have to do is follow the instructions on the screen. You'll need to input date, place, and GPS coordinates. There are history books about Pontiac's uprising in my office."

The professor's eyes moved back and forth nervously. "There are some things that you must remember. First, for safety reasons the Tuesday Teleporter will not allow you to return to this particular day in history again today. Second, my machine only works on Tuesdays. And, third, it will only go back to Tuesdays in time."

The professor hung up his headset. Then he turned the webcam toward where Robert was being held. We saw some movement on the screen as the professor walked toward the chiefs. Once again, the natives whooped and screamed as they held up knives and tomahawks.

This wasn't a movie. We shook with fear.

The native men grabbed Professor Tuesday and held him with Robert. Pontiac pointed at the two of them and spoke to his warriors. The professor looked scared.

Mr. La Blanc translated. "The native people are taking them hostage! The professor and Robert are being ordered to go with Pontiac's messengers."

The professor screamed as he tried to pull away. "I heard them say 'turtle,' look for us at Mi ..."

The professor's words were cut off. The next thing we heard was the sounds made by the teleporter. Then the green jelly thing just fizzled away. Robert and Professor Tuesday were nowhere to be seen.

"What do we do?" I asked.

"We go to work and try our best to save them," said Miss Pepper nervously.

Assignments

University Auditorium—Today

Mrs. Finch and Mr. La Blanc went to Professor Tuesday's office to gather up his history books about Chief Pontiac. While they were gone, Miss Pepper divided the class into work groups.

Miss Pepper pulled a whiteboard out from behind the stage curtains. She picked up a marker and turned to the work groups. "All right now," she said. "Before we begin our research, what have we learned from Professor Tuesday so far?"

Owen raised his hand. "The Native Americans liked the French, but they didn't like the British very much."

"Chief Pontiac is angry and wants to fight the British," Nathan added. "The British didn't give them gifts or help with trade like the French did. And, they were taking the native peoples' land."

Miss Pepper wrote notes on the whiteboard. "Good point," she said. "Keep going."

Rachel jumped up from her seat. "Neo ... Neo ... Oh, I can't remember how to say it. But, some spirit warrior told Pontiac that the Native Americans had to kick the British off their land."

"The professor said that Chief Pontiac was sending war belts to other tribes to join him in making war with the British," Louis said.

"Excellent," said Miss Pepper. "What were the last words we heard from Professor Tuesday?"

The class thought for a while. Then Madison spoke up. "He said that he and Robert were hostages and that they were going to be sent off with messengers to the other tribes."

"That's right," said Louis. "The professor also said something about 'turtle.' Then he said something else before he was cut off ... I think it started with a 'mi' sound."

"Very, very good," said Miss Pepper. "You've all been paying close attention. Now we're all going to work together to try to figure out how to save Robert and the professor."

Mrs. Finch and Mr. La Blanc handed out the history books they brought back from the professor's office. Some were very large. The work groups were given different assignments—studying Chief Pontiac and Fort Detroit; trying to figure out where Chief Pontiac may have sent his messengers;

identifying all the forts that were attacked during Pontiac's uprising; and looking for days and dates of the week when events took place. My group was assigned to find everything we could about "turtle" and what it meant.

Kelly raised her hand. "Miss Pepper, how are we going to find out which days in history were Tuesdays? And, what happens if we try to go on a Wednesday or a Friday?"

"I don't know just yet," our teacher said. "But I am confident that if we all put our heads together, we can figure these things out."

Miss Pepper cleared her throat before beginning. "Please think about your work group assignment and look through the books you've been given. I would like Mrs. Finch and Mr. La Blanc to join me at the stage for a moment. Then we will be around to help with your research." The adults had a private meeting while we set to work.

There weren't many pictures in the history book I had been given, just a lot of words. As I paged through the book, I looked up and watched the adults talking. Mrs. Finch seemed upset. Mr. La Blanc looked worried. Miss Pepper was very serious. After their meeting, the adults visited each work group to help. None of them looked too happy.

How would we ever find Robert and the professor?

Ottawa Village

Detroit, Michigan—
Tuesday, April 26, 1763

While we worked on our assignments in the auditorium, Robert and the professor were being held captive by native warriors in a time before the American Revolutionary War.

Some warriors took Robert and Professor Tuesday to the Ottawa village not far from the council meeting place. When they got to the village, they were put in a wigwam. The small house had a frame made of branches and was covered with bark. Inside the wigwam, there were few possessions. Deer hides lined the floor making comfortable beds. Outside, native men stood guard to prevent the two captives from escaping.

"This is terrible luck," said Professor Tuesday as he flipped up his sunglasses. "I always have pancakes for dinner on Tuesday. Now I'm sure I won't get pancakes for dinner tonight."

"Pancakes?" Robert asked as he looked at the professor. "We've been taken hostage, and you're worried about supper." Robert shook his head in disbelief. "Shouldn't you be thinking about a way to get us back home?"

The professor fumbled and trembled. "But I always have pancakes for supper on Tuesday. And, every day I have a tuna fish sandwich cut in two for lunch. What will I do?"

"Forget about pancakes and tuna fish sandwiches," Robert cried. "I've got a math test on Friday. If I don't pass it, my mom is going to ground me and take away my cell phone, video game, and TV privileges for a month."

The professor's eyes cleared and he burst out laughing. "If we don't get back to our own time, Robert, I won't get my pancakes and tuna fish sandwiches and you'll never have to take another math test. What's more," he added, "neither one of us will ever watch TV again."

The professor's sense of humor did little to comfort Robert. "How do we get out of here?" he asked.

"To tell you the truth, there isn't much we can do," the professor answered as he rubbed his forehead. "Your teacher and classmates have the Tuesday Teleporter. It's up to them to find us. If they can figure out what to do, we've got a chance to be saved. All I can tell you for sure is that we won't be rescued for at least a week. Until then, we'll have to figure out how to stay safe and out of trouble."

"Are we in danger, professor?" Robert asked.

"Yes, Robert," the professor answered, "we are in terrible danger."

Robert's eyes were wide with fear. The professor began to examine the inside of the shelter. There were no tools or weapons, just a few simple bowls and a dirt floor covered in animal hides. The wigwam had several holes. He thought about breaking through the walls to escape, but there were warriors guarding them. Besides, where would they go?

"Well," said Professor Tuesday, "I suppose we should take an inventory of the items we have with us."

"What do you mean, 'take inventory'?" Robert asked.

"We need to figure out what we have that might help us. Maybe we have some things that will convince the native people that we have magic," the professor said as he dug in his pockets. "Let's see. I have a pocket knife, some car keys, and a wallet." Then he reached into his white coat. "I've got some pens, gum, a watch, and a cell phone."

"A cell phone ... why don't we just call home?" Robert asked. "We'll be back in no time."

Professor Tuesday shook his head. "The towers that allow us to use cell phones won't be built in this area for another couple of hundred years or so from this time. Unfortunately, cell phones don't work if there isn't a cell tower nearby."

"Huh, I never thought of that," Robert replied.

Next, Robert emptied his pockets and back-pack. "I've got a backpack, some books, a couple of candy bars, and my gaming system. I've got some really cool war games if you want to play them."

"Not right now, thank you," said the professor. "It looks like we have some gifts we can give them. And, we definitely have some magic."

"Magic?" asked Robert, "what magic?"

"You'll see," said the professor. "For now, let's make sure the cell phone and the electronic game are both turned off. We'll need the batteries to be as full as possible if my idea is going to work."

Research

University Auditorium—Today

Back in the auditorium it was getting close to lunchtime as we set to work. Miss Pepper ordered some pepperoni pizzas while we silently paged through the old history books.

"I found something! I found something!" Madison said as she jumped with excitement. "I found a list of all the stuff that happened in Pontiac's war. It was in the appendix."

"Appendix?" Ashley asked. "My brother had his appendix taken out. He was in the hospital for a whole week afterwards."

"An appendix is a part of our body," Miss Pepper said. "However, the word *appendix* has another meaning as well. Many books have what is called an appendix. When authors write books, they often share information about related subjects.

They usually put this material in an appendix in the back of the book."

Madison held up her book. "This book has an appendix like Miss Pepper said. The title of Appendix B is 'A Chronology of Major Events.'"

"Very good," said Miss Pepper. "A chronology is a timeline of when things happened. What have you learned by looking at this appendix, Madison?"

"Chief Pontiac had his council meeting with other chiefs on Wednesday, April 27, 1763. Robert and Professor Tuesday were at that place on the day before—a Tuesday. The appendix shows that the next major event is going to be something called a 'siege' at Fort Detroit."

Ashley screwed up her face. "Miss Pepper, what's a siege?"

"Well, the word *siege* is a military term," Miss Pepper said. "A siege is when an army surrounds a fort. During a siege, those inside the fort can't get out to get food, water, and supplies."

"Oh," Madison said. "The siege at Fort Detroit is supposed to start on May 6. The appendix doesn't tell us what day of the week that is though."

"That's all right," said Miss Pepper. "We can count on a calendar to figure out what day of the week May 6 fell on in that year."

"There's a better way," Mrs. Finch spoke up. She held up her cell phone. "I've got the internet on my phone, and I found a web site that has a 'day of the week' calculator. If we plug in the date, month, and year, it will tell us the day of the week."

Miss Pepper was excited about the discoveries. "So, we know the dates when things happened, and we know how to find the day of the week. Now we need to try to find something about 'turtle.' And," Miss Pepper noted, "we need to figure out the GPS coordinates for the places we'll need to visit."

"GP what?" asked Louis.

Mrs. Finch went to a map. "GPS stands for Global Positioning System. On most maps, you'll see lines that go north and south. There are also lines that go east and west. The lines that go north and south are called 'longitude.' Those that go east and west are called 'latitude.'" Mrs. Finch traced the lines with a pointer.

"These lines are all numbered. Satellites orbiting the earth can locate any place on the planet using GPS coordinates. Cars that have GPS equipment use this information to help drivers find addresses in unfamiliar places. Many cell phones have GPS. If you are lost and have one of these phones, rescue squads can find you."

"Co-o-o-o-l," said Nathan. "So how do we find the numbers for the places that Robert and the professor might be?"

"I don't know just yet," said Miss Pepper. "But we must try if we are to rescue them."

Ottawa Village

Detroit, Michigan—
Wednesday, April 27, 1763

While we waited for our pizzas in the auditorium, back in history there was a huge commotion in the Ottawa village. Robert and Professor Tuesday had been in the wigwam for a full day and night. They were given dried meat to eat and water to drink.

"I'm hungry," said Robert. "Do you think we're going to get anything else to eat?"

Professor Tuesday didn't even hear Robert's question. "Today is the day," he said.

"Today is what day?" Robert asked.

"Chief Pontiac is holding his council meeting today with other war chiefs from the area. He will try to convince them to join him in his fight against the British."

"Are we going to see a real war up close?" Robert asked. His eyes were wide with excitement.

"I hope not," said the professor. "War is a terrible thing. This particular war will be cruel and very bloody. It will be nothing like the games you play on that little box of yours. Pontiac's uprising will spread across the Midwest. People on both sides will be terribly injured and many will die—British soldiers, traders, Native Americans—even innocent men, women, and children."

"Are we going to be okay?" asked Robert nervously.

"I honestly don't know, Robert," said the professor. "Hostages and prisoners were treated badly by both sides in this war. Some were even killed. But, we have two things working in our favor."

"What two things?" Robert asked.

"We know we are being sent with some messengers who will be carrying war belts to native villages," the professor said. "And, we have some magic."

"Magic?"

Just then the animal-hide door to the wigwam opened. A muscular native warrior waved Robert and the professor outside.

Professor Tuesday picked up his cell phone and turned to Robert. "Bring your gaming system with you, but don't do anything with it until I tell you."

They squinted in the bright light of day. Professor Tuesday flipped his sunglasses down to protect his eyes. A warrior spoke to him. The professor turned to Robert. "They speak Algonquin," he said. "I've studied the language for many years. He's telling us that we are his prisoners, and we must do as he says."

"I'm cool with that," Robert said, "as long as I don't have to do anything yucky."

The professor spoke to the warrior. The man then stood straight. The professor opened his cell phone and pointed it in the warrior's direction. 'Click,' he took a digital picture. After a moment, the professor turned the cell phone around to show the small picture on the screen to the native man.

"I-e-e-e-," shouted the warrior. Then he spoke excitedly to the professor. Other native people came running to see what was going on.

The professor turned to Robert. "He thinks I've captured his spirit. Don't show your gaming system yet, we can save that magic for some other time. I think we've given them enough of a show for now."

"You're right, Professor, we do have magic," Robert said as he watched the native people chattering excitedly and pointing at Professor Tuesday.

The professor turned to Robert. "Do you want to hear something funny?

"Sure," said Robert.

"Remember, my machine only works on Tuesdays and it only visits Tuesdays in history," said the professor.

Robert nodded.

"You and I are now living in this time, and today is Wednesday. So we have to spend at least a week here. And, it may take weeks or months living with these native people before your teacher and classmates finally rescue us."

"That's not funny," Robert said. "But Miss Pepper and my friends are smart. They'll rescue us soon. I'm sure of it."

That night, Robert and the professor feasted on smoked fish and wild berries. It wasn't pancakes, but it was pretty good.

As the sun set, the professor and Robert were taken to a wigwam to bed down for the night. Guards were placed outside the shelter to make sure they wouldn't escape. Robert sniffled softly in the dark.

"Is something wrong?" the professor asked.

"I want to go home," Robert said.

"We'll be rescued," the professor replied. "I know we will. You'll be back home before you know it."

"I know," Robert answered. "It's my fault we were captured. It's my fault that we're in danger. If I had paid attention and listened to your warning, we wouldn't be in this mess."

"We all make mistakes," the professor said kindly. "Now, get some rest, you need to keep up your strength."

Secretly the professor was worried.

Pieces of the Puzzle
University Auditorium—Today

The delivery man brought us pepperoni pizzas and soft drinks for lunch. Some of the pizzas had mushrooms, onions, and green peppers along with the pepperoni. We munched as we looked through the professor's books. Owen complained that he was allergic to green peppers. Ashley picked off the mushrooms and onions. Nathan ate the stuff that Ashley wouldn't. We were all concerned about Robert and the professor, but that didn't stop us from eating. Miss Pepper was too upset to eat. And, nobody laughed when Ashley burped.

As we finished our pizza, Ashley read about the different events that happened after Chief Pontiac's council meeting. "Okay," she said, "I already read about the siege of Fort Detroit on

May 6." Turning the page, she continued reading, "On May 16, Fort Sandusky was attacked and taken by native warriors."

"Fort Sandusky?" Owen asked. "That's where we visited earlier this morning?"

Mrs. Finch pointed out on the map where the different attacks took place.

Ashley lifted the heavy book and continued reading. "On May 17, Fort Miami was taken. It says here that Fort Miami is now called Fort Wayne, Indiana. Then on May 25, Fort St. Joseph was captured. That's near where Niles, Michigan, is today." Ashley hesitated. "Do you want me to keep going, Miss Pepper?"

"Yes, please—read a few more," Miss Pepper replied.

"I want to read," Rachel whined.

"Oh, all right," Ashley said, "you read."

Rachel gave a bratty smile and took the heavy book from Ashley. "On May 28, native warriors began a siege of Fort Pitt in what is now Pittsburg, Pennsylvania. Then on June 1, Fort Ouiatenon surrendered. That fort was where West Lafayette, Indiana, is now."

Mrs. Finch pointed to West Lafayette, Indiana, on the big map. "I went to college in West Lafayette, Indiana," she said. "That's where Purdue University is."

"Holy cow," said Sim. "It sure sounds like there were a lot of battles."

"There were many, many more," said Miss Pepper. "But that's enough for now. Did we hear anything that might give us an idea of where we could begin looking for Robert and the professor?"

"One of the forts was called Miami," Owen said. "That starts with a "mi" sound. Remember, like Professor Tuesday said before his computer shut off?"

Mrs. Finch got online and entered information into the day-of-the-week calculator. "The attack on Fort Miami happened on a Tuesday," she said excitedly.

"Miss Pepper," Manuel spoke up, "look at this. I found this paper in one of the professor's books. It's full of numbers that don't make any sense. The first line says Detroit 42.23 and 83.33."

The teacher rapidly walked up, down, up, down over to Manuel and took the paper from him. "This is it. This is what we've been looking for," Miss Pepper said as she clapped her hands in excitement. "Look," she said, as she showed the paper to the class. "Along the top of the page are the words LOCATION, LAT, and LONG. LAT is short for latitude, and LONG is short for longitude. These are the GPS coordinates that we need to find Robert and the professor. The professor must have written them down and left them in this book."

Miss Pepper congratulated Manuel and turned to the class. "You've all done a wonderful job of researching. Thank you all for your good work. Now let's hope we can find Robert and the professor."

The teacher did her up down walk all the way back to the stage. "The adults had a meeting before we started our research. We decided that it is too dangerous for everyone to go back in time to find our friends. So, Mr. La Blanc has agreed to search for Robert and the professor."

Louis looked worried. "No, Pops, you can't."

Mr. La Blanc put his hand on Louis's shoulder. "I've made up my mind. I want to help. Our family is French-Canadian, so I can speak a language that most of the natives will understand. Your teacher called the drama department here at the university. They'll be bringing over some clothes that were worn in the 1700s. I will look and sound just like a French trader." Mr. La Blanc ruffed up Louis's hair. "Don't worry, I'll be careful. Remember, Louis, we come from a long line of brave people. You must be brave now."

Moments later the auditorium doors flew open and in came several college students. They carried racks of clothing, shoes, and other stuff. Miss Pepper and Mrs. Finch picked through the items to find the right things. They gave them to Mr. La Blanc, and he went behind the curtain to change.

Some of our class started giggling when he came out. He wore a bright red shirt and trousers with a cloth belt. He had moccasins on his feet and a blue bandana on his head. Mr. La Blanc smiled broadly and took a big bow. We all clapped and cheered.

I couldn't help but thinking that there was a chance we could save Robert and the professor. But, what if Mr. La Blanc were captured, too?

Fort Miami

Fort Wayne, Indiana— Tuesday, May 17, 1763

Mr. La Blanc took his place on the stage in the auditorium as Miss Pepper entered the necessary information into the computer. She checked and rechecked the data several times. "Good," she said, "everything appears to be in order and working fine."

Mr. La Blanc looked out over the auditorium. "Don't worry about me, I'll be just fine. I will speak French to the Native Americans and Mrs. Finch can translate for you." He winked at Louis before continuing, "Everyone needs to stay in their seats. Understand? If the lights from the teleporter bother you, you can close your eyes now."

We shut our eyes tight as the professor's teleporter started lighting up and making its funny noises. After the lights stopped spinning and the humming sounds quit, we were surprised at what we saw on the big screen in the auditorium. Mr. La Blanc was walking toward a fort that was in the middle of the wilderness. Native warriors with clubs and tomahawks surrounded about ten soldiers. They pushed the soldiers into the fort and turned in surprise. They were shocked to see Mr. La Blanc and lifted their weapons as he approached.

Mr. La Blanc waved and called out to the warriors. Mrs. Finch listened carefully to what was being said.

"He just said, 'Hello, my name is Pierre La Blanc. I am a French trader.' Then he asked them if they were Ottawa or Miami." She listened as the warriors lowered their weapons and spoke. "The natives belong to the Miami tribe. They are greeting Mr. La Blanc as a friend."

Mrs. Finch focused on the screen as she listened. "They asked him if he has any powder or shot for their weapons. They have furs to trade." She listened as Mr. La Blanc answered. "Mr. La Blanc told them that all his goods have been stolen. Wait," she said. "He has just asked them if they have seen Pontiac's messengers."

One warrior stepped forward and waved his hands. As Mrs. Finch listened, a look of disappointment crossed her face. "He said that Pontiac's messengers arrived many days before. They have since gone back to their village."

We all sat on pins and needles as Mr. La Blanc continued talking with the warriors.

"He just asked the warriors if Pontiac's messengers were traveling with a young boy and an old man," Mrs. Finch said. A puzzled look crossed Mrs. Finch's face. "The warrior said that they were traveling alone. However, he also spoke of a strange old man with a spirit clam and his young companion."

"A spirit clam, what could that be?" Tyrell asked.

I shrugged my shoulders. "Beats me," I said. "But it sounds like some goofy thing Robert may have been carrying in his backpack. You know Robert."

Most everyone in my class nodded in agreement.

Mrs. Finch focused on the screen. Her lips moved as she listened. "Mr. La Blanc just asked the native where the elder and the boy were taken."

The warrior said only two words in French, "grande tortue."

Mrs. Finch put her hand over her mouth. She jumped up and down in excitement. "The warrior told Mr. La Blanc that Robert and Professor Tuesday were taken to the 'great turtle.' We just have to find out where or what that is. Then we'll be able to find Robert and the professor."

When Louis's grandpa safely returned from his travel into history, the class cheered and clapped.

"How was it? Were you scared, Pops?" Louis asked his grandpa.

"I was scared a bit at first," Mr. La Blanc admitted. "But, it was very exciting. They really believed that I was a French fur trader."

Louis was proud of his grandfather and gave him a big bear hug.

"We are getting closer," said Miss Pepper. "We know that Robert and the professor are alive. How do we find them? Where is this 'great turtle'?"

"Miss Pepper," Rachel asked, "what do you think the native man meant when he said the strange old man had a spirit clam?"

"I don't really know," the teacher replied.

"Miss Pepper! Miss Pepper!" I shouted in excitement. "The book I've been given says that a Delaware chief named Turtle Heart was at the Pennsylvania provincial store on May 27, 1763. Turtle Heart and his warriors seemed to be in a hurry to trade their furs and hides. The book says they bought as much gunpowder and shot as they could. Then they left the village and went to the river to join the Shawnee Indians as they prepared for battle at Fort Ligonier."

"Good job, Jesse," Miss Pepper said. "Professor Tuesday has GPS coordinates for that place on the paper that Manuel found. What else have you learned about this Chief Turtle Heart?"

As I made my report, Mrs. Finch entered information into her cell phone. "May 27 was a Friday," she said.

"That will never do," Miss Pepper said. "We need to find a Tuesday."

"Wait," said Louis. "If Turtle Heart was trading furs for bullets and stuff on Friday, they must have been visited by Pontiac's warriors earlier in the week—maybe on Tuesday."

"Excellent thinking, Louis," Miss Pepper noted.

"I don't like this anymore," Tamika said. "I'm scared."

The Great Turtle

Off Point Au Gres, Michigan— May 20, 1763

While we were living in modern times, Robert and the professor were in a canoe on their way to the great turtle. The day was a warm one for the month of May. Pontiac's warriors paddled the canoes holding their captives through Lake Huron, making good time.

"Dude, these guys are buff," Robert said as he paddled. "I don't think I can paddle any more. My arms are so tired; I think they're going to fall off."

"I beg your pardon?" asked the professor.

"I said that these warriors are muscle men," Robert replied. "They can sure paddle a canoe. How far do you think we are traveling in a day?"

"I'd guess we are covering about forty or fifty miles each day," said the professor as he looked around at the scenery. "This is a beautiful area of what is Michigan in our time. We're just off Point Au Gres." The professor pointed up the shoreline. "By the end of the day, we should easily make what will be Tawas or Oscoda in the future."

Robert chewed on a piece of dried meat. "Where do you think they're taking us?"

"We are going to the land of the great turtle," said Professor Tuesday. "That is what the native people call Michilimackinac. In our time we call the area of Michigan Mackinaw City and Mackinac Island."

"How did it come to be called the great turtle?" Robert asked.

"Well," said the professor, "when you look out on the water from Mackinaw City, you can see Mackinac Island. The island looks very much like a turtle. So the area became known among the natives as the great turtle."

"Awesome," Robert said. "I've been to Mackinaw City. My family took a ferry to the island and water shot out the back of it, high into the air. We even took a horse-drawn carriage ride there." He thought for a minute before continuing. "Why are we traveling all this way by canoe? Wouldn't it be easier for us to go by road? My legs are cramping and my bottom is getting sore from being in this canoe for days on end."

The professor smiled as he responded to Robert. "In the 1700s, there are no roads or bridges like in our time. The roads and highways you've ridden on won't be built for centuries. It would take us much longer to make this trip over land. Plus, it would be much more uncomfortable. We would have to cut our way through thick forests and terrible swamplands. The bugs can be bad on the water, but they are much worse inland."

Robert scratched at his bug bites. "How much longer will it take us to get to this 'great turtle' place?"

Professor Tuesday thought for a moment. "For natives in canoes, it generally took about ten days from Detroit, give or take. So, I'd guess we'll be there in a couple of days."

Robert stopped paddling for a moment. "What do you suppose they'll do with us when we get to Michilimackinac?"

"I don't know for sure," said the professor. "I can tell you that the Chippewa and Sauk Indians will attack Fort Michilimackinac on June 2. It will be a terrible battle and many will be killed, mostly British."

A serious tone came over the professor's voice. "Pontiac's messengers suspect that we are British because of our clothing. There is no telling what they'll do to us." The professor's eyes looked to the clouds. "We do have magic to help us, however. I only hope it will be enough."

"Maybe I could spook them with my gaming system," Robert said. "We may have to use that magic to save our lives."

"Good thinking, Robert," said the professor. "Now you're using your noodle."

Robert wondered what his "noodle" was, but he didn't ask the professor what he meant. They paddled through the day. Occasionally, native men, women, and children would appear along the shoreline and shout greetings. The warriors shouted back.

By the end of the day, the canoes were pulled ashore near the mouth of a small river. As a cloud of mosquitoes descended on the party, one warrior passed a wooden bowl to Robert.

"Great," Robert said as he reached for the bowl, "I'm starving."

"Don't eat that," the professor shouted as he grabbed Robert's hand. "That's a mixture of grease and clay. The natives use it to keep the bugs away."

Robert looked at the professor. "I'm glad you said something." Then he smeared the mixture on himself. "Phew ... this stuff really stinks."

Delaware Village

Near the Pennsylvania Provincial Store—May 24, 1763

Back in modern times, we were working hard to save Robert and the professor. After an afternoon snack in the auditorium, all our preparations were completed. Mr. La Blanc took the Tuesday Teleporter back in time to the Delaware village where Turtle Heart lived. The village was very quiet. A few men gathered about. Dogs chased and played between the bark-covered wigwams. Women prepared food and worked around the village. Young native children ran between the huts squealing and playing their games.

Mr. La Blanc placed the webcam near the green gob that was hidden in the brush. He whispered into the microphone, "I'll hide here in the trees until something happens."

We were all excited. Everyone knew we were getting close to Robert and the professor. However, Miss Pepper looked worried. It was getting late in the day. She was responsible for all her students, not only Robert. Once again, Mr. La Blanc was putting himself in danger.

The bus was scheduled to pick us up at twenty minutes past two in the afternoon. That was only thirty minutes away. "Hurry, Mr. La Blanc, hurry," Miss Pepper whispered so that none of us could hear. "Please bring everyone home safely."

The auditorium was quiet. We could hear the clock ticking. Louis was nervous and chewed his fingernails. Sure, he was worried about Robert and Professor Tuesday, but he was mostly concerned about his grandpa.

At five minutes past two, there was a commotion in the village. "They're here," Mr. La Blanc whispered into his microphone. "The warriors who just arrived are Pontiac's men. They look like the natives we saw in Detroit." Louis's grandpa stepped out from behind the trees and walked to the village.

"Bonjour amis," said Mr. La Blanc.

The native men responded in French. Mrs. Finch translated as they spoke. "Mr. La Blanc said 'Hello friends.' The native men said 'Who are you'?"

Louis's grandpa and the native warriors talked for a while, and then Mrs. Finch spoke. "Mr. La

Blanc told the native men that he has traveled a long distance looking for an old man with a spirit clam and a young boy who were with Pontiac in Detroit." Mrs. Finch listened very carefully. "He told them that he had heard the two were being taken to the grand turtle, so he came to see Turtle Heart in order to bargain for their release."

The native men threw their heads back in laughter.

"Oh, no," said Mrs. Finch. "The natives told Mr. La Blanc that Robert and the professor were not traveling to Turtle Heart but to the place known as the great turtle, Michilimackinac."

Just then, things went from bad to worse. Chief Turtle Heart pointed at Mr. La Blanc and said something. Two warriors ran to him and took him by the arms, lifting him completely off the ground. Louis's grandpa looked scared as they carried him away. "They think I'm a spy," Mr. La Blanc shouted. The warriors threw him roughly into a wigwam in the center of the village.

Louis cried out, "No, Pops, no!"

"No, not again," Miss Pepper cried. Then she gasped as she looked at the clock. It was quarter past two. The bus would be arriving any minute. Now three people are lost in the past—Robert, Professor Tuesday, and Louis's grandpa.

Miss Pepper and Mrs. Finch huddled together. They talked in fast whispers. Miss Pepper's face was white with fear as she turned to face us.

"When the bus arrives, Mrs. Finch will help you get back to school and to your homes safely. I will stay here and do all I can to rescue our friends."

"No way," said Louis. "I'm staying right here until my grandpa comes back."

The class mumbled and grumbled. "We all want to stay, Miss Pepper," Ashley said. "Can't we stay and help for just a little longer?"

"Wait, look," said Madison as she pointed at the screen.

Our attention turned to small movements at the back of the wigwam that held Mr. La Blanc. A panel of bark began moving. After a bit, Mr. La Blanc's head poked out of the rear of the shelter. He looked around to make sure no one was watching. Then he wiggled out of his prison.

Before Turtle Heart and his warriors noticed, Mr. La Blanc crept quietly away from the wigwam. As he approached the webcam, his arm reached across the lens. In the blink of an eye, Mr. La Blanc approached the teleporter and stepped through. When he finally stood on the stage once again, Louis shouted for joy.

Miss Pepper ran over to Mr. La Blanc – up, down, up, down, up, down. "Are you all right?" she asked.

"Yes, thank you. I'm fine," he said. "Now we know for sure where to find Robert and the professor."

"Mr. La Blanc," the teacher said. "You've just been captured. You could have been killed. We can't take any more chances. I can't let you go back in time again. It's just too dangerous."

Mr. La Blanc crossed his arms. "Miss Pepper, we know for certain where to find Robert and Professor Tuesday. We can't leave them." He let out a sigh. "The professor's teleporter only works on Tuesdays. If we don't bring them back today, then we'll have to wait a whole week before we can try again."

He waited a few minutes to let his words sink in. "The longer we wait, the more danger they may be facing. Besides, what are you going to tell Robert's parents? We've got to save them now."

The Final Clues

University Auditorium—Today

The auditorium was quiet, but I had just found something. I quickly raised my hand and jumped up and down in my seat.

Miss Pepper called on me. "Jesse, have you found something you want to share?"

"Yes, Miss Pepper," I answered. "Here's what I found in one of the professor's books: Fort Michilimackinac was taken on June 2, 1763." I looked up at my teacher before continuing. "It says here that a group of Chippewa and Sauk was playing a game called—called," I stumbled with the word, "I don't know how to pronounce it."

"Please spell it out loud," Miss Pepper said.

"B-A-G-G-A-T-I-W-A-Y."

"Baggatiway," said the teacher.

I continued, "They were playing a game of baggatiway in honor of the king's birthday, King James I of England." I stopped for a moment and thought out loud, "Do you think that baggatiway is the game like lacrosse that Professor Tuesday was talking about this morning?"

"I believe so, Jesse," Miss Pepper said. "Please keep reading."

"The players ran back and forth chasing a ball with long-handled nets. The game was being played just outside the gates of Fort Michilimackinac."

"If the native people were playing sports, we'll find Robert right there in the middle of it," Nathan said.

Miss Pepper nodded at me to continue reading. I turned the page and started up again. "During the game, native women wrapped in blankets gathered near the gate of the fort. No one wondered why these women wore blankets on such a hot June day. Underneath their blankets, they hid knives, tomahawks, and other weapons."

I liked reading aloud almost as much as reciting the Pledge of Allegiance. "The game was very exciting. Most of the soldiers, including the commander of the fort, were watching. At one point in the game, the ball was tossed inside the gate of the fort. As the players went after it, they dropped their nets and took the weapons that were hidden under the women's blankets."

Mrs. Finch spoke up. "I'm sorry to interrupt, but June 2, 1763, was on a Thursday."

Thank you, Mrs. Finch," said Miss Pepper. "If the attack on Fort Michilimackinac happened on a Thursday and we go there on the Tuesday of the same week, we may just find Robert and the professor there."

"Miss Pepper," Owen said. "I've got a book written by a man named Alexander Henry. He was at Fort Michilimackinac when it was attacked."

"Yes," the teacher said. "What did you find out?"

Owen swallowed hard. "It says that almost all the British who were at Michilimackinac were killed in the surprise attack. Those who weren't killed, including Alexander Henry, were taken prisoner. Some of the prisoners were even killed later."

I gulped. "It doesn't sound too good for Robert and the professor."

The teacher covered her eyes as she thought. Then she turned to Mr. La Blanc. "Are you ready to do this one more time?"

Mr. La Blanc gave Louis a big hug and then nodded. "Let's do it."

At that very moment, the bus driver showed up in the auditorium. "All right, Arrowhead students, it's time to go."

Miss Pepper looked around nervously. "No, not now. We can't leave without Robert and Professor Tuesday."

"We want to stay, Miss Pepper," Owen said.

"Not me," said Tamika "This kind of scares me."

Just then, lights began flashing. A robotic voice came from Professor Tuesday's laptop, "Tuesday shutdown in thirty seconds." The voice continued, "The computer will shut down for one week in twenty seconds." Sirens began screaming from the speakers in the auditorium. "Shutting down, NOW!"

Miss Pepper looked confused. She went to the laptop. Miss Pepper frantically pushed keys on the computer, but she couldn't re-start it no matter what she tried.

The bus driver spoke up, "Miss Pepper, I've got a schedule to keep. We'll have to leave right away."

"I'm sorry," Miss Pepper said to the class as she straightened her clothes. "I understand that everyone is scared for Robert and the professor. But, we must all go back now. The professor's laptop has shut down until next Tuesday, and there's no way to get it to work now. We can't keep the bus driver waiting, and I don't want to worry your parents. This is getting far too dangerous. I will call Robert's parents and talk to the people at the university before I go home for the day."

Our teacher looked very frightened as she continued, "If Mr. La Blanc and Mrs. Finch are willing, we will all come back next Tuesday and try our best to save Robert and the professor."

"We'll be here," said Mrs. Finch. Mr. La Blanc nodded in agreement.

"So will we," I said. "We've all worked hard to save them. We want to help."

Everyone in the class shouted in agreement. It was too bad that Robert and the professor weren't going home today, but we all felt hopeful as we got on the bus. They were both very smart. They could take care of themselves. We were smart, too. If we all worked together, we could save our friend and the professor next Tuesday.

At least we thought we could save them.

Arrival at Michilimackinac

Mackinaw City— Monday, May 30, 1763

It was a clear, calm day as the canoe carrying Robert and the professor glided through the waters near Fort Michilimackinac. As it approached a native village, the canoe turned toward land. Just before the craft reached the sandy beach, the native warriors jumped out and pulled the canoe safely ashore.

"Are we at the Great Turtle now?" Robert asked.

Professor Tuesday pointed toward the small island that appeared to be a few miles out in the big lake. "There is the Great Turtle. The native people believe that the island is home to the Great Spirit. So, this entire area is very sacred to them."

The warriors directed Robert and the professor to the village, and the natives living there looked on curiously. They had been traveling eleven days. Robert and the professor had spent the entire time in the same clothes. Their shirts and pants were torn and tattered. The professor's white lab coat was now dirty and stained. His beard and hair were mussed and matted.

The group stopped in the center of the village. There the native women looked over Robert and the professor. One of the women took the professor's glasses off and put them on herself. She cried out when the sunglasses popped up. Then she jumped as she threw the glasses to the ground. When the professor bent over to pick them up, a distinguished looking native man stepped forward. One of the warriors who guarded the time travelers said one word, "Wawatam."

"Oh, thank goodness," said Professor Tuesday in relief. "Robert, my friend, we are very lucky indeed."

"Huh?" Robert asked.

The professor and Wawatam spoke in French. All the while, Robert's eyes followed their conversation back and forth. Though he couldn't understand a word that was being said, he saw the two of them smiling as they talked. That was a good sign—a very good sign.

After the visit with Wawatam, Robert and the professor were escorted to a wigwam and given some food. They were both hungry and tired from their long trip.

"So, who's this Wawatam dude?" Robert asked.

"He's no ordinary dude," said the professor. "You and I have just been in the company of a very brave and wise man. Chief Wawatam is an Ojibwa chief. He was one of the very few Native Americans who tried to save people in the attack that will happen later this week."

"Oh, I remember," Robert said. "You said that the Chippewa and Sauk Indians will attack Fort Michilimackinac on June 2. That's only a few days from now."

"Very good, Robert," said the professor. "Chief Wawatam himself will help one famous British merchant, named Alexander Henry, to survive the attack on the fort."

"That's good, I suppose," said Robert.

"There's more," the professor continued. "He promised that he would help to save us during the attack."

"Whew," said Robert, as he pretended to wipe sweat off his forehead. "Then we're safe."

"Not just yet," the professor replied. "Chief Wawatam is an important leader. But, many of the warriors and war chiefs who have come to this place are very angry with the British. Wawatam's influence may not be enough to save us when the time comes."

"Then what do we do?" Robert asked.

"We prepare our magic in case we need to use it," said the professor. "Are the batteries still good in your gaming system?"

Robert dug the game out of his backpack and flipped the power switch. After tapping the bottom screen with the stylus, a war game came to life in his hands. Suddenly, the thought of playing war was not much fun to him. After he checked the battery and made sure it still held a charge, Robert turned off the game and shut the lid.

"The battery's good," Robert said. "How can we use it to make magic?"

"Well," the professor began, "Chief Wawatam told me that you and I are valuable prisoners. By now, your classmates have probably figured out where we are and how to find us. If my guess is right, they will try to rescue us tomorrow … on the Tuesday before the attack on the fort."

"And?" Robert asked.

"And, we may have to use every bit of magic we have to escape from the angry warriors. Pay close attention and be prepared to show your magic when I give you the sign."

"We've got to get out of here," Robert said as he shook his head. "I want to go home."

"I want pancakes and a tuna fish sandwich cut in two," the professor said with a nervous smile.

Looking for Friends

Fort Michilimackinac—
Tuesday May 31, 1763

Miss Pepper had a terrible week. The school principal, Mr. Blackhurst, was very angry that she had taken her students on a field trip and came back to school with one student missing. The president of the university, Dr. Clayton, was angry at Professor Tuesday, blaming him for Robert's disappearance. Robert's mom and dad were also angry. However, they were angry with Robert for not paying attention on a field trip. No one was happy.

The next Tuesday, Miss Pepper and her class showed up at the university auditorium early in the morning. Mrs. Finch and Mr. La Blanc were there. Robert's mom and dad took seats near the stage. Dr. Clayton took a seat in the back of the auditorium. And, our principal, Mr. Blackhurst, stood by Miss Pepper as she entered data into the professor's laptop. It was clear that she didn't like him looking over her shoulder. I crossed my fingers, hoping that everybody would be safe and happy by the end of the day.

Mr. La Blanc was dressed like a voyageur. He took his place on the stage as Miss Pepper checked the data on the professor's laptop one more time. Our teacher and principal stepped back from the teleporter. We closed our eyes as the colored lights began whirling and sounds circled around the auditorium.

After the Tuesday Teleporter created its green gob that floated in the air, Mr. La Blanc took a peek inside. Then he stepped through with the webcam and a microphone head set.

The webcam moved around a bit before settling on a view of a native village. Beyond the village, we could see a stretch of blue water. Mr. La Blanc pointed a finger at a spot nearby and spoke softly, "In our time the Mackinac Bridge will be standing right there."

"Whoa," said Natalie, "I've been over that bridge."

"Me, too," said Kelly. "I even ate fudge right at the spot were Louis's grandpa is now."

Miss Pepper checked her wristwatch nervously. It was twenty past nine in the morning. She hoped that Mr. La Blanc would find Robert and the professor quickly. Mr. Blackhurst was anxious. Dr. Clayton was upset. And, Robert's parents were nervous and eager to get their son back. Everyone stared at the screen, hoping to see something soon.

Mr. La Blanc walked toward the village. The camera he carried bounced with every step he took. When he got close, Mr. La Blanc put the webcam down on a log. It was a beautiful day with a bright blue sky. The leaves on the trees were rustling just a bit. We could see a thin line of smoke coming from the village.

The wigwams that formed the village were little round huts covered in bark. Strips of meat hung from sticks over a small fire nearby. No one tended the fire. No natives were to be seen. All was quiet.

Mr. La Blanc whispered into his microphone, "Looks like nobody's home."

Suddenly, a ball fell out of the sky and landed on the sand right in front of the webcam. The quiet was broken by the sounds of children shouting. The screen quickly filled with images of bare feet and legs running toward the ball. There was a lot of shoving. Sticks smacked against bare legs. In the scuffle, the leather ball was gathered up in a small net and tossed toward the village. Children ran toward the ball and continued their rough game.

"Is that?" whispered Mr. La Blanc. "Yes, it is! It's Robert!"

As the group scrambled for the ball, one player stood out clearly from the rest. He was about a head taller than everyone else, but the other players were faster. His clothes were ragged and tattered and his face and arms were dirty. Yet, it clearly was Robert digging and fighting for the ball with the native children.

"There's my baby," Robert's mother cried. "Oh, look at him. He needs a bath."

We all looked at her funny. Then, when we turned back to the screen, Mr. La Blanc was walking with the webcam toward the players. As he got close to the group, he called out Robert's name. The game continued and he called out his name again, louder this time. Suddenly, Robert stopped and looked up. When he saw it was Mr. La Blanc, he dropped his stick and ran toward him.

"It's you! It's you! You're Louis's grandpa," Robert said as he hugged Mr. La Blanc. "You found us. Professor Tuesday was right, today would be the day that you'd rescue us."

Mr. La Blanc took Robert by the arm and headed toward the teleporter. "Let's go back, everyone's been worried sick about you."

Robert pushed away from Mr. La Blanc. "I can't go back, not now. We've got to wait for the professor."

"No," said Mr. La Blanc firmly. "You and I are going back right now."

Miss Pepper shook her finger and shouted at the screen, "Robert, you get back here this instant."

"You listen to your teacher," Robert's mother shouted. "Get back here now."

Nobody but Mr. La Blanc could hear what was being said in the auditorium. If we weren't so scared for Robert and the professor, we would have all had a good laugh. We all sat on the edge of our seats as Robert continued to argue with Mr. La Blanc.

"I won't leave the professor," Robert said. "He saved my life. I won't leave him behind. I won't!"

"Where is he?" Louis's grandpa asked. "I'll go get him."

"He's having a meeting with Chief Wawatam," Robert said. "He'll be back soon, I'm sure of it."

"We'll wait for a few minutes," said Mr. La Blanc. "But we can't stay long—you are in great danger."

Waiting for Tuesday
Outside Fort Michilimackinac—
Tuesday May 31, 1763

As they waited near the village, Robert talked to Mr. La Blanc about everything that had happened since his capture near Fort Detroit. We all listened carefully. "Chief Pontiac had his warriors take us prisoner. It wasn't much fun. As we were led away, the professor tried to tell you exactly where we were going."

"He was cut off just as he was saying 'Michilimackinac,'" Mr. La Blanc said. He shook his head slowly. "Your classmates worked hard, researching everything they could about Pontiac's uprising. They are the ones who found you."

"That's awesome! Thanks, guys," Robert said to the class through the microphone. "They kept us in a small wigwam for a few days. We didn't get anything to eat but jerky and water until Professor Tuesday showed the natives our magic."

"I wanted to talk to you about that," said Mr. La Blanc. "I met with some native people and they told me that they knew of a young boy who traveled with an older man who had a spirit clam. What was that all about?"

Robert laughed aloud. "Dude, that's hilarious. Professor Tuesday took pictures of several natives with his phone. They thought he was capturing their spirits." Robert thought for a moment. "I suppose a cell phone looks like a clam. That's it," Robert said as he snapped his fingers. "The professor did have a spirit clam."

Robert thought for a while before speaking again. "Professor Tuesday is pretty smart. Everything changed when he started taking pictures of the natives with his cell phone. I guess they thought we were magic guys or something. Anyway, after that we started getting better food and treatment."

"What did you eat?" asked Mr. La Blanc.

"Man, they make a stew with deer meat and corn that is totally rad," Robert said.

"What?"

"Oh, sorry," Robert continued. "I meant to say that the stew was fantastic. Though Professor Tuesday sure did miss his pancakes and tuna fish sandwiches."

"Oh," said Mr. La Blanc, "I understand now."

"When we got here to the 'Great Turtle,' Professor Tuesday met this Chief Wawatam guy. Anyway, the professor told me that Chief Wawatam was a very famous and powerful Native American chief. The professor also said that Chief Wawatam promised to help us to escape the attack on Fort Michilimackinac. It's supposed to happen on Thursday, you know. That's only two days away."

"I know," said Mr. La Blanc. "That's why we have to get out of here right now."

Suddenly the webcam caught some movement down by the lake. A group of natives were walking toward the village. Professor Tuesday's bald head poked out above the crowd of native people.

Robert turned toward Mr. La Blanc. "They know me. I'll go get the professor. You stay here."

Mr. La Blanc started to argue, but he knew Robert was right. Robert ran toward the village and took Professor Tuesday by the arm. They were too far away to understand what they were saying, but the professor looked very excited.

Professor Tuesday turned toward the natives, waving his arms as he spoke. The natives looked angry and took hold of both Robert and the professor. Professor Tuesday called out for Chief Wawatam, but the chief was nowhere to be found.

Warriors tied the hands of Robert and Professor Tuesday and began to lead them away.

"I don't like the looks of this," Mr. La Blanc gasped into the microphone.

"No, no!" Miss Pepper said.

We were all too shocked to say anything. Robert's parents held each other tightly. Mr. Blackhurst chewed his fingernails nervously. And, Dr. Clayton had a scowl on his face as he paced back and forth at the rear of the auditorium. We'd almost rescued Robert and the professor, now we weren't sure we'd ever see them again.

"What do we do now?" I asked.

Before anyone in the auditorium answered, Mr. La Blanc's voice came over the speakers, "I'm going after them." Then Mr. La Blanc picked up the webcam and placed it on his head.

"Don't do it, Pops. Come back," Louis cried.

Nathan went to Louis and put his arm around him. "Don't worry about your grandpa, Louis. He is very brave and very strong. I am sure they will all come back safely."

The webcam followed Mr. La Blanc's movements as he stormed toward the village. When he came upon the warriors who were holding Robert and the professor, Mr. La Blanc used a commanding voice as he spoke to them in French.

Mrs. Finch approached the screen and translated as Louis's grandpa spoke to the warriors.

"Mr. La Blanc told the warriors to let Robert and the professor go," Mrs. Finch said. The native men then spoke to Mr. La Blanc. They sounded angry. "They are questioning Mr. La Blanc. They want to know who he is."

Before Mr. La Blanc could answer, the warriors took hold of him. Soon he was tied up alongside Robert and the professor.

Things were going from bad to worse.

Magic

Outside Fort Michilimackinac— Tuesday, May 31, 1763

The webcam stayed on as the warriors seemed to be arguing. Mrs. Finch's lips moved as she translated the French they spoke.

"One warrior wants to do them harm," Mrs. Finch said. "Others want to let them go. The warrior is claiming that Mr. La Blanc, Robert, and the professor are British spies."

Mr. La Blanc said something that made the warriors stop arguing. Mrs. Finch listened carefully to each word. "Mr. La Blanc offered to be their prisoner if they would let Robert and the professor go free."

Everyone in the auditorium sat in silent shock. Louis just stared forward with a terrified look on his face. Miss Pepper's heart sank with worry.

"Wait," Mrs. Finch said. "Someone else is speaking now."

The camera that Mr. La Blanc was wearing turned and came to focus on Chief Wawatam. The native chief walked up to the crowd around the prisoners and spoke with authority.

A smile crossed Mrs. Finch's face as she listened to the French spoken by Wawatam. "The chief is ordering the warriors to let them go."

The auditorium erupted in cheers and applause.

Mrs. Finch's face turned sour. "Wait, wait. The leader of the warriors refuses to free the prisoners." Her lips moved and worry crossed her face. "He is saying that the others should not listen to Wawatam, that the chief is old and weak ... someone who cannot be trusted because he likes the British."

Everyone in the auditorium slumped. It was not looking good.

Chief Wawatam stood up tall and pointed his finger at the prisoners. "He is saying that the warriors are holding magic men ... men who are strong with the Great Spirit."

A few of the warriors laughed. They did not believe what Wawatam was saying. The chief himself walked up to the three prisoners and removed the knife from his belt. He then cut them free.

"Chief Wawatam ordered the prisoners to show their magic," Mrs. Finch said.

The professor made a great show of removing his cell phone from his pocket. Through his travels, he had taken great care of his phone for just this moment. Professor Tuesday held the phone at arm's length and tried to take a picture of the warrior.

There was no click. Nothing happened. The professor's cell battery had gone dead.

Professor Tuesday showed the blank screen to the warrior anyway. The warrior pushed the cell phone aside and glared at the prisoners before speaking.

"The warrior said that the professor's spirit clam was a trick. He won't let them go," Mrs. Finch said.

Professor Tuesday nodded to Robert. And, we sat on the edges of our seats as Robert stepped forward.

Robert knew what he had to do. He took his gaming system out of his pocket and turned on the power switch. Music played as it started up. The warriors all took one step backward in fear. When Robert took out the stylus and started shooting bad guys, the warriors covered their ears and ran.

Mr. La Blanc quickly led Robert and the professor away from the village and toward the place where the teleporter was hidden.

"Get us out of here," the professor said nervously. "Now! Now!"

In a matter of moments, Mr. La Blanc, Professor Tuesday, and Robert were riding the swirl of colors and sound. In no time, they stepped through the teleporter and were back in the auditorium unharmed. The professor wilted to his knees. "Somebody, get me two aspirins and a glass of water quickly. Then I want a hot bath and some pancakes for supper. But, if you can find a tuna fish sandwich, I'd like that now ... cut in two, please."

The class cheered and jumped up and down. Mrs. Finch left the room to fetch some water. Miss Pepper ran down to the stage to help the long lost travelers.

Lessons of History
University Auditorium—Today

Robert's parents ran up to give him a hug. His mother laughed and cried at the same time. His father looked proud.

"Sweetheart, did you get a chance to brush your teeth?" Robert's mother asked.

Robert just rolled his eyes.

I cupped my hand over my mouth to keep from laughing.

The professor took two aspirins and drank a full glass of water. Someone from the university cafeteria even delivered his favorite lunch, a tuna fish sandwich cut in two. As the travelers rested, they talked with Miss Pepper and Mrs. Finch. Before everyone left the auditorium, the professor rose to talk.

"I, for one, have learned a great deal over these past days," the professor stated. "In fact, I have gathered information that will be the foundation of a wonderful new research paper ... a paper that will undoubtedly add to the honor and prestige of this fine university."

Dr. Clayton's frown quickly turned into a smile. New research on the native peoples of the Midwest would be good for the university and a feather in his cap. Even Mr. Blackhurst looked proud and happy that Miss Pepper had saved the day without any lasting harm being done to anyone.

Professor Tuesday looked out at us in the auditorium. "I have heard from Miss Pepper, Mrs. Finch, and Mr. La Blanc that you are the ones responsible for our rescue," the professor said proudly. "You are excellent students and I want to thank you all for your good work."

The professor continued, "So, what have you learned from what happened?"

"We learned that many of the native tribes were angry with the Europeans who moved here, especially the British," Rachel said.

"True, true," said Professor Tuesday. "Many of them liked the French, mostly because they felt the French treated them better than the British."

Nathan raised his hand and the professor called on him. "Pontiac and the Woodland Tribes defeated a lot of British forts."

"Very good, very good," said Professor Tuesday. "By the time Pontiac's uprising was over, only three British forts in the Midwest remained untaken—Fort Detroit, Fort Niagara, and Fort Pitt." The professor hesitated before continuing, "You might be interested in knowing that shortly after Fort Michilimackinac was taken, Fort La Baye—the place we visited when you first came to the university—was abandoned by the British."

"What ever happened to Fort Detroit?" Lucy asked.

"Well," the professor said, "Chief Pontiac and his warriors surrounded Fort Detroit from May to November in 1763. Pontiac decided to stop the siege in order to take his people to their hunting grounds. He did this so his people would survive the harsh winter months ahead. Because he and his warriors never actually took Fort Detroit, many native people turned on him. Some tribes and warriors even hated him."

The professor took two sips of water before continuing. "Many believe that Chief Pontiac could have defeated the British at Fort Detroit. He commanded more than 800 warriors, many from the Saginaw Bay area. Pontiac did not attack Fort Detroit even though his warriors outnumbered the British. It is likely that he did not attack because he didn't want to lose warriors in the fight."

"What happened to the native tribes who fought against the British during Pontiac's war?" I asked.

The professor shrugged his shoulders twice. "In July of 1766, three years after the uprising began, Chief Pontiac and other western chiefs agreed to a treaty with the British. Under the terms of the treaty, the natives acknowledged the King of Britain as their 'father.' They also promised to return all the hostages they had taken. Plus, the native chiefs promised to make war on all tribes who broke the peace with their British brothers."

"What did the British promise to do?" Natalie asked.

"The British pardoned Chief Pontiac and the others who were involved in the uprising," the professor replied. "They also promised to remove white settlers from the lands of the native people."

"So, what happened after the treaty?" Louis asked.

"True to his promise, Chief Pontiac became a loyal supporter of the British," Professor Tuesday noted. "But, as I said, Pontiac was very unpopular with many other Native Americans. Maybe it was because he became a strong supporter of the English. Anyway, he was killed by a Peoria Indian in Illinois in 1769."

The professor shook his head. "Though Pontiac and most other native chiefs kept their promises, the British did not. They did not stop settlers from moving onto native lands."

The professor thought for a moment before continuing. "European peoples with their vast numbers, technologies, and their colds and diseases moved in and eventually pushed the native peoples off their land. Through history, most of the promises that were made to the native peoples were broken."

Robert spoke up, "I learned how Native American people lived and cared for each other. They fought for what they believed in and did what they could to protect their families and lands. Each member of the village had a job to do, and they worked together. They even loved sports."

"Did you learn anything else?" asked the professor.

Robert looked down at his shoes. "Yes, I learned that I need to do a better job of paying attention. If I had listened, I wouldn't have caused this big mess. I am sorry and want to thank Professor Tuesday, Mr. La Blanc, Miss Pepper, and everybody in class. You guys are the best."

Robert shrugged his shoulders before continuing, "My mom and Miss Pepper are always trying to get me to put down my game and read more. So, I think I'm going to spend some time with books ... history books mostly. History is awesome, and the professor's Tuesday Teleporter is cool."

Miss Pepper and the whole class started clapping.

"Wait," said Robert as he was being led from the stage. "There's more. I want to thank Professor Tuesday for all his help and I'm really glad he'll be able to have pancakes for supper tonight …"

THE END

Author's Notebook

1. **Historical Fiction**—*Chief Pontiac's War* is a story that is classified as historical fiction. While it is based on history and contains many historical facts, several situations and the modern characters in the story come from the author's imagination. Can you name three characters in the story who are historical figures and three who are fictional, or made up?

2. **Creating Your Own Historical Fiction**—Write a story about your last birthday. All the people in the story should be real characters. However, create a character to represent you. As you write your story, describe how your fictional character feels at different points during the day. Try to create a few different conversations between the fictional character and the real characters.

3. **Professor Tuesday and Miss Pepper**—The names for the professor and the teacher come from the author's imagination. However, the good professor was named after a real person. Although the person's true name is not "Tuesday," the person seems to always say that he'll get something done on Tuesday. In creating Miss Pepper's name, the author wanted a unique name that made the reader think of someone with a spicy character. Can you think of some unique names for characters in an adventure story?

4. **The Narrator**—Much of the story is told through the eyes of Jesse. Describe Jesse in your own words. Is Jesse a boy or a girl? Is Jesse wise or silly?

5. **Jargon**—Jargon is defined as terminology or language that is used by a group, activity, or profession. People who enjoy gaming often use a particular type of jargon. Doctors usually speak in medical jargon. Can you name a group of people who have their own jargon?

6. **Voice**—Different people speak differently. Children speak differently than adults. Teachers usually speak differently than dentists. Mothers often speak differently than fathers. When writing a story, authors have to pay attention to the voices of their characters ... how words and phrases are used by unique characters. See if you can point to how Miss

Pepper's and Robert's voices are different in this story.

7. **Passenger Pigeons**—During one point in the story, the class sees a huge flock of passenger pigeons. Research the passenger pigeon and write a report on the bird. Include in your report a description of a passenger pigeon (including your own drawing); estimates of how many passenger pigeons there were thought to be at one time; what the passenger pigeon ate; and how the passenger pigeon became extinct.

8. **Character Development**—When writing a story, it is fun to develop the personalities and behaviors of different characters. Describe these different characters in your own words: Miss Pepper, Robert, Professor Tuesday, Mr. La Blanc, Tamika, and Louis.

9. **Surprise**—Surprise is an important element in any story. Did anything happen in the story that surprised you? Did you find a funny surprise? Did you notice any scary surprises?

10. **Onomatopoeia**—Words that imitate sounds are referred to as onomatopoeia. Zoom, pow, and bang are a few examples. In this story, a native man trades for a gun. The guns used in the 1700s were called flintlock rifles. When a flintlock rifle is shot, it makes two distinctive noises. First, it makes a CLICK when a piece of flint creates a spark. Next, it makes

a BOOM when the gunpowder in the rifle is ignited. Can you think of some words that make sounds?

11. **Homonym**—Words that have more than one meaning are often referred to as homonyms. For example, the word 'left' can mean your left hand or left side. 'Left' can imply that someone or something was left behind. In this story one of the students locates an 'appendix' in a book. Another student thinks 'appendix' is a part of the body. Both are true. The word 'appendix' is a homonym. Can you think of another homonym?

12. **Native American Tribes**—*Chief Pontiac's War* mentions several different Native American tribes. Research the tribes in your area of the country. Find three facts about one of the tribes and share these facts with your classmates.

13. **Location**—In the story, the students discover the GPS locations for different places. The author of this story lives near the 45th parallel. Do you know what the 45th parallel is? What is it between?

14. **Historical Places**—Several historical places are mentioned in this book. They include Fort Detroit, Michigan; Sandusky, Ohio; Fort La Baye, Wisconsin; Fort Michilimackinac, Michigan; and several others. Write a story about visiting a historical site and what you learned when you were there.